The Quiet River

By P. M. Hubbard

The Quiet River

P. M. HUBBARD

PUBLISHED FOR THE CRIME CLUB BY

DOUBLEDAY & COMPANY, INC.

GARDEN CITY, NEW YORK

1978

All of the characters in this book
are fictitious, and any resemblance
to actual persons, living or dead,
is purely coincidental.

Library of Congress Cataloging in Publication Data

Hubbard, Philip Maitland, 1910–
   The quiet river.

   I. Title.
PZ4.H8772Qi 1978 [PR6058.U2]   823'.9'14
ISBN 0-385-14244-7
Library of Congress Catalog Card Number 77-27709

*To my old and dear friend Delia Stockford,
whom I have never met.*

The Quiet River

Chapter 1

The river, when they came to it, was bigger than they expected and much less beautiful. It was big only by the standards of minor English rivers well inland from the coast—they were not expecting the Mississippi, or even the Severn—but it was still unexpectedly big. It was a smooth, unbroken body of brown water moving steadily through the flat green country, and running in so slight a curve that it looked almost artificially straight, as if it were a canal. It must have been all of twenty-five yards across from bank to bank, and the banks were steep. They could not tell how deep the water was, but it looked deep.

There were no frills at all, no islands or backwaters, no lilies or bullrushes—not even, as far as they could see, any trees growing on the bank. The fact of the river was there in front of them, but all the pleasant associations their minds had conjured up were missing. They stood for a moment looking at it in silence, and then the whole smooth surface was suddenly pock-marked with spreading rings, and it began to rain. They still stood there, turning up their coat-collars and trying to find words to say to each other, but no words came, and the rain went on, falling straight out of the grey sky onto the brown, dimpled water. It was difficult enough to know what to say without having the rain beginning to soak into their clothes and run down their necks, and presently they gave it up and turned and went back to the car.

They shook off what water they could and got into their

places, and Steve started the engine and turned the heater on. He ran his window down so that the damp off their clothes would not steam up the windscreen. It was not cold outside, and the rain fell so vertically that none of it came in. He said, "So that's Lod. Pity we had to see it like this." He always called rivers by their bare names, without the definite article, as if they were people, but even he was not going to pretend that the Lod was not to some extent a disappointment.

Helen said, "It's bigger than I thought. I don't know—I wasn't expecting more than a good-sized brook." It was the size of the river that impressed her more than its lack of charm. She had been thinking of a human amenity, but this was something you would have to live with, like a mountain at your back. Once you had seen it, it dominated the landscape from underneath, as a mountain dominates it from above, only, unlike a mountain, you did not see it at all until you were right on top of it. It must run, obviously, where the contours of the ground dictated, and it had dug itself into its present channel, but there was nothing like a river-valley to show you, from a distance, where it did run. You knew it was there, snaking its way along the line of least resistance, but most of the time, like a snake, you did not see it. It was a river, right enough, even in some way quite a formidable one, but she knew at once that it was not her idea of what a river should be.

Unexpectedly, perhaps because he was sensitive about rivers, Steve answered what was in her mind rather than what she had actually said. He said, "It'll look better when the sun's out. And it's a nice piece of water. Clean, too. There's no reason why it shouldn't be, coming from where it does. One could swim in it without poisoning oneself, and there ought to be fish. It's not a pretty river, I admit, but it's real, and it hasn't been mucked about with. I think I could get to like it." But then Steve did like rivers. He called them by their Christian names, if Lod was Christian, which she doubted. To Helen it was the Lod, and she did not think she was going to like it whatever she called it. But perhaps that did not matter very much, and in any case there was nothing she could do about it.

She said, "It's not pretty, certainly, but I've nothing really against it. It's just that it isn't what I was expecting, and I don't somehow take to it."

He nodded. "Well, look," he said, "let's leave it out of the reckoning. It's not the asset we hoped for, but I don't think it's a liability either. Let's forget it's there, and make our decision on all the other things. The house mainly, I suppose, and that's really up to you. We had to see Lod, and we've seen it. Let's go back and have a proper look at the house."

She said, "All right, I agree," because there was nothing else she could reasonably say. She knew he would not openly force her hand. But she knew already that he wanted the place, and she did not think, now, that she did. As for forgetting the river was there, she could not, any more than he could. Already, even from here in the car, it was out of sight again, but she knew very well it was there. Steve backed and turned the car on the rough grass, and they bumped back along the track to the road.

The house was called Spandles. It stood on a spur of slightly higher ground that reached out from the low hills behind it, and looked southward across the flat fields towards the invisible river. The fields went with the house. They stretched for perhaps a quarter of a mile each way along the bank. There were a few lines of thorn hedge, but mostly the fields were divided only by posts and wire. The individual fields had no natural identities, because there was nothing in the shape of the ground to give them any. It was really one big field broken up for practical purposes, and the fences had an arbitrary, almost temporary, look, like the electric fences the farmers used to control grazing. Even the big field itself was almost rectangular, bounded by the almost straight river to the south and an almost straight road to the north. East and there were just the thin fences stretching between road and river. The house would have been a farm-house once, and could be again, but now the grazing was let to the farmer along the river. If they took the house, it would be only the house they would have to worry about, and the bit of garden that went with it. That was what had attracted them, that and the river. Steve was no farmer and had no intention of being one, but he liked rivers.

The house was pleasant enough, but not dramatic. You could not expect drama in that landscape. It was built of brick, rendered over and colour-washed in a flat buff, so that from a distance it looked like a stone house, but there was no building stone in these parts. There was a walled kitchen garden east of the house, and here the brick walls had been left uncovered and did not look amiss. In front, southwards, there was a small open garden of grass and flower-beds, which had been terraced out from the end slope of the spur, so that from the front of the garden there was a vertical drop of seven or eight feet to the fields below. There was a brick retaining wall here, with brick steps in the middle going down to the fields, and the wall ran back along both sides of the garden until, about half-way along, the level of the garden merged with the level of the higher ground where the house stood. Behind the house there was an open yard between out-buildings, and from there a drive led through a wooden gate to the road running east and west thirty or forty yards away. Westward the house was open to the green fields and a distant view of Calton Farm, which was where Mr. Summers lived. It was Mr. Summers who had the grazing of their fields, or what would be their fields if they took the house. They had not met Mr. Summers yet. They drove in through the gate, open now because there was nothing to shut in or out, and parked the car in the yard.

The rain had stopped and the sky was brightening minute by minute. There was no wind at all, but the sun was breaking through the thin cloud cover, and presently they would have a hazy sunshine. There was a tremendous feeling of air and space, and it was dead quiet. Even here there were no trees, just the man-made verticality of the buildings breaking the flat landscape. It was all extraordinarily peaceful, but the peace had a brooding quality that you would have to accept if it was not going to worry you. When the wind blew, there would be no defence against it, but it was not a windy part. It was too far from the sea for that. In the winter there would certainly be snow, but snow, as England gets it, is not great menace in a flat country. Placed as they were, Helen could see that the house had a lot to offer them.

Steve took the house keys out of the pocket in the dashboard, and they got out. They had already had a quick look at the house, and then Steve had wanted to go and have a look at the river. Now they must make a proper job of it, and they both knew that it was Helen who had to make up her mind. Steve was already committed.

They went in by the back door, because that was the door they would nearly always use and everybody always had. The front door opened on nothing but the flower-garden, and the side door on nothing but the kitchen-garden. It was the back door that was the real entrance of the house. A narrow hall ran right through from back door to front door with two rooms opening out of each side of it and the stairs going up between the two western doors. Half-way along the hall, between the back rooms and the front, there was a glazed door. It was open now, hooked back against one wall, but it would be a useful draught-stopper when the wind blew. All four rooms had windows in both outer walls. One of the back rooms was the kitchen, but the others, stripped and empty, were theirs to do with what they liked. It was a simple, unimaginative plan, but not unpleasing, and the rooms were high and light, with tall sash windows. They went into each of them in turn, silent as it were by consent, each making his or her own judgement. As they went into the second front room, the light suddenly brightened, flooding in from an outside world that seemed all sky, and touching the bare boards and faded wallpaper with a pale yellow glow. It was a solid, reassuring house, that would hold no secrets, and for a house that had been shut up so long, it smelt unexpectedly sweet.

It was the sweetness that decided her, even before they went upstairs, that and the sudden flood of pale sunlight in the empty rooms. She still did not like the river, but you could not see it from here, and it seemed a long way off. Even now she did not say anything, but she knew what she was going to say. As they came back into the hall, Steve said, "Say about 1850?" and Helen nodded.

"Something like that," she said. "Let's see upstairs." She started up the stairs and he went after her. Their shoes clumped on the bare boards, but the risers were low and the stairs easy to climb. As if conscious of the noise they made, he fell into step with her, two stairs lower down, and they walked steadily up in unison, clump, clump, clump, so that anyone listening in one of the upstairs rooms would have thought there was only one person coming upstairs. But there was nobody, of course, to worry with the noise their feet made on the treads, only three nearly square rooms, as bare as the rooms below them, and full of the same soft sunlight from the same tall windows, and the plumbing concentrated over the kitchen, to save piping and heat.

There were not so much views from the windows as outlook. It was like looking out of a lighthouse. But you could see the low hills north and south, and eastwards, farther away but higher, the jumbled hill-country where the river water collected itself for its long run westward to the sea. Even from this height you still could not see the river itself. She wondered why she was as conscious of its presence as she was when it was so extraordinarily good at hiding itself, and then thought that perhaps it was just because you could not see it that you had to keep on telling yourself that it was there. But she had surrendered now. The house had got her, and to hell with the river. The house could be lovely, and she knew she could make it look better than it had ever looked yet.

When they had gone into all the rooms and come out again on to the central landing, she turned to look at Steve, because she knew he was watching her, and when she smiled at him, his face crumpled into a smile of such enormous relief that he looked for the moment ridiculously young. "It's nice," she said. "I like it."

"Oh good," he said. "I like it very much myself. What do you think?"

"Well look, we're only proposing to rent it, not buy it."

"At this stage." Steve interrupted her deliberately, smiling and making a joke of it but quite determined now to make her understand how much he wanted the place.

"All right, at this stage. But I mean—there are a lot of things we don't really have to worry about that we should if we were buying it. We're not putting capital into it. All we're investing is the expense of the move, and of course we'll have to do it up a bit. But it's not all that much of a serious decision. Do you want a survey?"

He shook his head quickly and decisively. "No. That's one of the things we needn't worry about. The structure's obviously sound, and if the house has got any vices, we'll discover them as we go along, and no real harm done. I'd get the plumbing and heating checked, but that's all." He said "I'd," not "I'll." He was still determined not to seem to assume her agreement, and she had not agreed yet. But he had made up his mind. He was only playing reasonable.

Now she did agree. "All right," she said, "go ahead and take it."

He looked at her with a curious solemnity, which she was to remember later. "You're sure? You're not agreeing against your better judgement?"

She found herself irritated by his insistence, because her

decision was not too firmly based, and now that she had made it, she did not want to have to take another look at it. And she knew that the balance in her mind was different from his, almost its opposite, because she liked the house and disliked the river, but she did not want to tell him that. She said, "I don't know about my better judgement. But I'm sure, yes. You go ahead, and let's see what we can make of it."

There was a window in the south wall lighting the landing from behind him as he stood and faced her, and now, as they looked at each other, a flicker of movement caught her eye through the bottom pane, and she took her eyes from his and looked past him to the field in front of the house. "There's someone there," she said, and he turned, and they stood looking out together. There was a man coming across the field towards the steps at the bottom of the garden. Even from up here he looked immensely tall and thin, and he walked with a deliberate, swinging stride. His clothes and hat were uniformly black, so that he made a surprising figure on the sunlit grass, as if he were a scarecrow walking. They watched him until he came to the steps, and even then his head and shoulders remained in sight, and the next moment there he was at the top of the steps, taller than ever, looking up the garden towards the front of the house.

Instinctively they both moved back, so that he should not find them watching him if he looked up at the first-floor windows. Helen said, "Come on. Let's go and see who it is," and they hurried down the stairs together, not worrying now about the noise they made. Steve ran into the kitchen and came back with the keys, looking for the one labelled for the front door. It was a formidable piece of ironmongery, and when they turned to the inside of the door, they found a massive box-lock, with a touch of what had probably been brass decoration, but had long since been painted over. The key turned with a smooth heaviness and the bolt thudded back on a powerful spring. Even then they found the door bolted top and bottom, and Steve wrestled with the bolts, swearing softly under his breath. He got them drawn at last and stepped back and swung the door open, and there was the tall man standing almost on the threshold, not more than a couple of feet from them, and looking down at them, first at Helen and then at Steve.

He was much less disconcerted than they were, because he had been standing there listening to Steve's fight with the door, and they had not known where he had got to. He said, "Ah good morning. Mr. and Mrs. Anderson?" He spoke as deliberately as he moved, and his voice was very deep and curiously vibrant, despite the narrow, bony chest. His whole manner gave an impression of age, which his face and body belied. The face was smooth and almost rosy, with large dark eyes staring down at her, and when he put his hand up and solemnly raised his hat, Helen saw that his hair was as dark as his eyes. He could not be more than forty, and might even be less. He was a good head taller than Steve. She found him more impressive at close quarters than he had been at a distance, which in her experience was uncommon. He said, "My name's Summers. I was told you were coming to see the place. I hope you like it?"

He spoke to Helen, but it was Steve who answered. He said, "We do, yes. We've just decided to take it."

"Ah. That's good." He seemed to bow slightly to each of them in turn, and Helen had a feeling that he was going to raise his hat again, but he did not. She wondered whether she ought to ask him in, but that was absurd, because there was nothing to ask him in to, and in any case it was not their house yet. He said, "Spandles has been empty too long, and that's a fact." His speech puzzled her. There was a touch of the locality in it, but he did not speak like a farmer, nor yet like a professional man. It had a sort of formal, almost ceremonious, courtesy, so that she wondered for a moment whether he had been at some time a superior servant, a butler or something of the sort, in one of the great houses of the neighbourhood, only here he was farming, and she had never heard of a butler turned farmer. In any case, he did not seem old enough.

Steve said, "How long, in fact?"

Mr. Summers said "Seven years." He did not hesitate, or qualify the figure. It was as if he had it very much in the front of his mind, and was even waiting for them to ask. "That is," he said, "it will be seven years in a few months' time since Mr. Wetherby died."

Something turned cold suddenly in Helen's mind. She could not swear, looking back at the thing afterwards, that she had known what was coming, but she had known something was. Steve did not seem to be aware of it. She did not look at him, but he spoke in a perfectly ordinary conversational tone of voice. He said, "Ah he died here, did he?"

"That is so," said Mr. Summers, and then once more he corrected himself. "That is," he said, "not actually here in the house. He was drowned in the river."

Chapter 2

The trouble was that the thing was not mentioned between them until a good deal later, quite late in the evening, when they were back at their hotel in Skrene and had had their dinner. At the time they had gone on with their curious, formal conversation with Mr. Summers, standing there together in the hall, with the sunlight streaming in past them, and Mr. Summers towering between them and the bright sky behind him. They had all three cast long shadows on the dusty boards of the hall, but his shadow had been longer than theirs. Helen remembered this afterwards, because at one moment the back door, which they had left open, had shut itself gently behind them, probably because of some imperceptible movement of air from the open front door. She had turned instinctively at the sound, and had seen, but only remembered afterwards, that Steve's shadow and hers were blended into one indeterminate shape, whereas Mr. Summers' went past theirs in a long streak down the hall, with his head and odd black hat foreshortened but still recognisable at the end of it. They had talked about the use of the fields, and the shopping, and the water-supply, and local communications, and all the things a local can tell a new-comer about life in the neighbourhood, and he had offered to supply them milk direct from his farm, in its natural state, before it had been, as he put it, mucked about with at the dairy. He had seemed anxious in every way to make them welcome, but as it were in principle, without much feeling of personal liking, or even of any particular mental contact. She had remained curiously impressed by him, but above all puzzled, as if all the real qualities in him, the things you like or dislike in a person, were somehow out of sight, so that she could not make up her mind whether to like him or not. Steve had been slightly amused by him, but she had not felt any amusement, for all his obvious oddity, only this uneasy feeling of reserved judgement.

He had made his formal farewells after a bit, and lifted his dark hat from his dark head, and turned and gone off down the garden, and then Steve had shut the door just before he reached the steps, in case he should turn before going down and see them still watching him. The bolts were easier now, and Steve bolted and locked the door and dropped the bunch of keys into his pocket. With Mr. Summers finally and conclusively shut out, he turned and said, "Funny chap. But he seems to want to be a good neighbour. I wonder if he's married. He didn't mention a wife."

That was the moment when she should have taken her stand. It would not have been difficult then. She could have said, "Steve, I've changed my mind. I don't think really I'm going to like it here. Let's go on looking." He would have been disappointed, even a little angry, but she thought he might have accepted it and asked no reasons. Whether he would have known the reason she could not tell. On the face of it its very unreasonableness seemed to make it unlikely that he should, but the trouble was that because of its unreasonableness she felt guilty about it, as if she would be crossing him for a mere whim, and when she felt guilty about a thing, she always had the feeling that he must know about it. She often wondered what she would have done if she had found it necessary to deceive him systematically, even in fairly unimportant matters, as many of her friends deceived their husbands regularly for the sake of peace in the home. If he did know her reason, he would know how unreasonable it was, and then if later they came to regret their not taking the house, he would, at least in his own mind, hold it against her, and she could not risk that.

So she said, "I don't think he's married, no. I can't think what sort of a wife he'd have," and Steve had looked at her for a moment and then laughed.

"Can you ever tell?" he said. "Look at the sort of people people do marry."

"Yes, but there are still people who don't marry, and not for any of the obvious reasons. I rather see Mr. Summers as one of them."

He laughed again. He was full of pleasure and excitement at the decision they had come to, and he would have laughed at almost anything she said. "Well," he said, "you'll have plenty of chance to find out." She nodded and smiled, because she did not want him to think she took Mr. Summers too seriously, but she was conscious of a twinge of something very like despair, and of an undisguisable touch of resentment, because not for the first time she had left something unsaid that she had needed to say, and knew now that she would never say it.

It was only when they were undressing for bed that Steve said suddenly, "You know—that house is in pretty good shape for one that's been empty seven years." He had been reverting to the house and the place again and again throughout the evening, so that she had the feeling that, even when they were talking about something else, the main part of his mind was still occupied with it.

She said, "Not quite seven years. A few months more to go," and then was surprised that she had kept this in her mind and had bothered to correct him on it. He stood there in his singlet and underpants, with the shirt he had just pulled over his head dangling in his hand. He made a pleasant, uncomplicated figure, fair, reasonably hard, straight up and down, undramatic but perfectly satisfactory. But he still stood there looking at her, and she realised that he had found what she had said puzzling, and was still waiting for the answer he expected. "Oh yes," she said, "I agree. Surprisingly good. It didn't even smell stuffy."

He nodded and turned and threw the shirt over the chair where his other clothes were already draped. He was not the sort of man who folded his clothes up overnight. He said, "And poor old Mr. What's-his-name drowned himself in Lod."

"Wetherby," she said. She did not usually remember names, but she had remembered that one, and the very way Mr. Summers had pronounced it, with his curious preciseness and yet that touch of burr in the *r* that a Southeasterner would never have given it. She may even have echoed his pronunciation a little when she herself said it.

Something, either the tone of her voice or the unusual accuracy of her memory, must have got through to him, because he came over to her suddenly and put a bare arm round her bare shoulders and pulled her against him. "Look, my sweet," he said, "people do drown in rivers occasionally, and always have. There won't be a stretch of any river in England that hasn't had a drowned man in it at some time, any more than there's a yard of English ground that hasn't got a dead man somewhere in its make-up. It's an old country, and people have been dying all over it for a long time. It's not a thing to worry about. For myself, I prefer it that way."

She leant against him, suddenly desolate and in desperate need of assurance. "I know," she said, "I know. But then you like rivers. I don't think I do awfully. And I wish it hadn't been our immediate predecessor."

She was willing him with all she had in her to make the move that she herself had failed to make earlier, or at least to give her a second chance by admitting even the possibility of reconsidering their decision, but he did not do it. He said, "Seven years isn't all that immediate," which she knew was nonsense, but did not challenge because it was irrelevant to the main issue, and on the main issue for the second time she had given way without a fight. He was holding her tightly to him now, and she knew that he was going to make love to her because he felt happy and assured, and wanted to drive his assurance into her until she surrendered to it. She would surrender, because she always did, and now the thing was settled irrevocably, and they would take Spandles, and she would no doubt learn to live with the invisible river, just as she had learned to live with everything else, including Steve himself. She put her face up to be kissed, and surrendered herself with a sort of eager desperation to an assurance that she knew would hold her for the moment but knew equally would not last.

Next morning, before they set out on their drive home, he said, "Anything else you want to look at while we're here? There's not all that rush to get away." She noticed the "else" and put her own interpretation on it. She did not in fact want to see the house again on this visit, still less the river, but in any case the words he used were clearly meant to exclude any reconsideration of what they had seen and decided the day before. Whatever had been true then, it was no longer true that if she were to come out against the place now, he would accept her change of mind without a fight. He had not even any intention of giving her a chance of raising the matter. He was determined to hold her to her decision, and would use every means of persuasion he possessed—including the oldest one in the book, she thought bitterly, and then was frightened by the sudden, unexpected bitterness of her thought.

Meanwhile she looked at him with an expression of mild consideration on her face. Then she said, "I'd like to have a look at the village, I think," and he was all compliance at once.

"I agree," he said, "let's do that. It's not far."

The village was westward along the road that ran behind the house. It was called Ladon, and the map showed a lane leading directly from there to Calton Farm, where Mr. Summers lived. If you went from one house to the other by road, you would go through Ladon. Otherwise you could walk directly through the fields along the river, as Mr. Summers had walked the day before. They themselves had come from the east, and had turned off into Spandles, while Ladon was still a good mile ahead. But for better or worse it would be their village, and a village can be very important. However much they seemed to be committed to the house, it made sense to see it.

Today again they came from eastwards, and when the house showed up on their left, Steve slowed down a little, but not enough to suggest that he was thinking of turning into the drive. It was another windless morning of hazy sunshine, and Spandles stood up square and almost golden on the verge of the higher ground. It was as they came round the last slight bend in the road and had the house full in view that she suddenly caught her breath and all but exclaimed aloud. If she did not exclaim, it was because she was already on her guard, conditioned, even in the last twenty-four hours, to the concealment of her feelings on the whole subject. The house stood up in the quiet sunshine, but below and in front of it there was nothing, only an unbroken sheet of soft brightness, so that for a moment she thought the river was already at their doors. In another moment she saw what it was, but the knowledge did little to reassure her. The whole stretch of the valley lay under a sea of mist. She could not tell where the far side of it was, but it seemed to lap their garden steps, so that if Mr. Summers had come that way today, he would have emerged suddenly from under the mist, like some uncouth sea-creature coming unexpectedly ashore. Somewhere out in the middle of it, always invisible and now doubly concealed, the river ran through the damp fields and fed the mist that covered them. She felt suddenly that she was going to shiver, and moved sharply in her seat, covering the involuntary movement with a calculated one. Then they were past and the house dropped behind them, and still neither of them spoke. They drove on in silence for the remaining mile, and when they were into the outskirts of the village, Steve said, "Here we are," in a perfectly ordinary, cheerful voice, so that she would never know whether he had seen what she had seen, or known at all what she felt about it.

The village was as solid and ordinary as the house, and like it built entirely of brick. Some of the bigger houses were pargeted as Spandles was and others were colour-washed straight onto the brick. In only a few cottages the brick had been left untouched. Among all this brickwork only the church was of stone and the garage was of concrete with an iron roof. The houses and a few shops were strung along both sides of the road, with yards or small gardens behind them, and half-way along there was a crossroads with a pub on the corner. The road that went left would be the one that went to Calton Farm and probably ended there. There was nothing to say where the other one went to. The church stood back from the north side of the road. Like many such, it stood a little higher than the rest of the village, but in this flat land the difference looked very slight. There were a few cottages and some new bungalows for a short distance along both side roads, and that was all there was of the village. They drove slowly through it from end to end, and then Steve stopped and turned the car. "Let's park somewhere and walk round," he said.

She nodded, and he drove back into the village and pulled the car into the side just short of the crossroads. There were footpaths on both sides of the road, but seemed to be very few people about. The children would have been swept off in buses to their schools, and the grown-ups would be working, out in the fields or in their houses. The village sat there, unwelcoming but at their disposal, in the quiet sunshine. They got out of the car on their different sides and stood there a moment, looking up and down the street. Then Helen said, "I'm going to do the shops. What about you?"

"I'll try the pub," he said. "I'll ask if they can give us coffee. It's always a test, whether they do it, and if so, how. They won't know who we are yet."

She looked at him, as she sometimes found herself looking, almost with incredulity. He was wrong both ways, of course. He quite unaffectedly thought he was somebody, and she did not think he was. And he thought the village would not yet know them as the people likely to take Spandles, whereas quite obviously it would and did. It was only the second point she felt up to arguing. "They will," she said. "Like to bet? Mr. Summers knew, and was even expecting us."

"He's different. They'd have had to tell him because of the grazing. After all, we might have wanted the land with the house."

Helen shook her head. "Bet you a quid," she said. "But you'll have to play fair and tell me what they say."

He smiled at her. He was still very cheerful. "A quid it is," he said. "I promise I won't cheat." He set off walking towards the pub, and she crossed the street, because two of the shops were on the other side, and walked parallel with him, on her side, towards the crossroads at the centre. By the time she had crossed the side-street, he was no longer in sight.

Both shops knew who she was and said the proper things, but the whole effect was a little disconcerting, as if they welcomed her arrival as a fact rather than her as a person. There was interest, certainly, even a degree of curiosity, but no feeling of personal sympathy or even personal contact. It was Mr. Summers all over again, only with Mr. Summers her own interest had been aroused, whereas with these people she could not be bothered. They were not hostile, and she supposed their attitudes might change with time, but the idea of settling down among them appalled her. She came out of the second shop, still saw no sign of Steve and then, on the impulse, dodged into a narrow opening between two houses and made for the church gate. A paved footway ran level from street to gate and then, still on the same alignment, rose slightly from church gate to church porch. But the rise was slighter even than she had thought from the street. The church floor might be a couple of feet above the floors of the nearest houses, but that was all there was in it.

The date cut into the buttress at the corner of the porch caught her eye as she was going in, and she turned aside to look at it. There was no inscription, just a neat horizontal line cut across the face of the stone and the date 1837 above it. It was about a foot above ground level. She looked at it for a moment but could make nothing of it. Then, as she turned back towards the church door, an explanation occurred to her, and she swung back to look at it again. Her eye went from the line cut in the stone down to the village street and then, through a gap in the houses, out across the flat fields towards the river. The mist had gone now. She could see the fields all right—Calton fields, they would be by now—but still not the river. The distance seemed enormous, but even over the distance the difference in height need not be all that great.

The voice behind her said, "Don't worry. We don't get many like that," and she spun round to find the woman watching her.

Chapter 3

The pub did not give them coffee, but Steve paid Helen a pound on their bet. He said, "They knew who we were, all right." He offered no further details, and she took her money and asked no questions. She thought he was less than happy with his reception, but would rather pay up than admit it. She knew exactly how he had been received, because it would be in the same way as she had been received herself, and it would not satisfy him. They drove mostly in silence, but so they usually did, and in their different ways both preferred it. Like other men she had known, Steve took his driving seriously, as if it were an end in itself and not merely, as it was to her, a means of getting from one place to another. She could not complain of his actual performance. He was a highly skilled driver, not unduly thrusting, but competitive and sharply critical of others. She had a car of her own, but never drove him in it. When they travelled together, they travelled in his car, and he did all the driving. What would happen if on some occasion they both had to use hers she did not know, but so far the occasion had not arisen. As it was, he concentrated all his attention on his driving, and she retired willingly into her own mind, where she found herself increasingly comfortable. It was not what she had once expected of marriage, but it could have been a lot worse. His egotism was entrenched but not aggressive, and he could turn on the charm like water from a tap. He had married her because he saw her as the sort of wife a successful author ought to have, but she had known this even at the time. She had married him because he could give her the security she had very badly needed, and was sufficiently civilised and attractive to make the thing viable. In a sense it had been a marriage of convenience on both sides. She had no complaints, but was becoming increasingly aware of the dangers.

What she mostly thought about was the woman in the churchyard. She did not know her name, because women who met casually did not feel the same compulsion to exchange names as men did. For men it seemed to be an essential part of the process of establishing not only their identity but even their actual reality, as if there was no certainty that an unnamed man really existed. Helen did not know the woman's name, but her existence was already the most important thing she knew about Ladon. The next most important was the existence of Mr. Summers. She knew his name because, being a man, he had produced it himself, but the woman, being a woman, had not. She assumed from what she had said that she lived in the village, and that was the most important fact about her, because, being the woman she was, her mere presence there had profoundly changed Helen's attitude to the place. She thought she was congenial, but, congenial or not, she was real, a single point of reality in what had threatened to be a world of total unreality. Mr. Summers' reality had yet to declare itself, but she was fairly certain it was there. Whether, when it did declare itself, it would be congenial she could not tell, but at least his promise of reality gave him importance. She had an uneasy feeling that this need for people who were real might reflect in some way a growing apprehension that Steve was not. At any rate, the need was there, and she had to live with it just as she had to live with the possible reason for its existence.

Oh yes, the woman had said, the river flooded regularly, as in that landscape it was bound to, but the 1837 level was the record to date. There had been a lot of work done on the

river since then, and it was a long time now since it had
even reached the village. Mostly it was just the fields on
both banks. It made them wonderful pasture, but no good
for arable, because it was important to leave the turf undisturbed. Calton Farm, the actual buildings, stood lower than
the village, though there was lower ground still in between,
and the farm could on occasion be dry itself, but cut off, but
never for long, and even then a tractor at least could get
along the road. The floods came and went quickly, throwing
off in one rush any excess of rain that had fallen in the high
country eastwards. Spandles was in fact the highest point
for some miles round, except possibly the church itself,
higher than both Calton and the village. But the differences
were hardly noticeable to the eye. It was the water that
showed them, when the water came. No one seemed to
know what had happened at Spandles in 1837, but the village had not been threatened in living memory, and that
went back a long way. The house had been re-built after
1837, but not because of any flood damage, just as an ordinary piece of modernisation. "You'll be all right at Spandles," the woman had said, and Helen had said, "Mr. Wetherby wasn't," and the woman had looked at her and said,
"Who told you that?"

"Mr. Summers."

"You've met him?"

"Yes. He came to the house yesterday when we were
there."

The woman had nodded. Then she had said, "Old Wetherby wasn't at Spandles. He was in the river. Nothing to do
with a flood. There wasn't a flood that year."

"How did he get into the river, then?"

"I don't think anyone knows. He may have been fishing. I
know he was a fisherman. He was just found downstream
before anyone had noticed he was missing here. No one saw
what happened. Or that's what I gathered. But Spandles is
safe enough."

Then Helen had gone off to meet Steve, who would be wondering where she had got to, and when she had met him, she had not mentioned the woman in the churchyard at all, or even the flood-mark on the church porch. There was after all no reason why she should. If the woman had told her that Spandles was liable to flooding, it might have been different, but she had said it was not. As for the flooding of the fields, Steve had probably guessed that already, even if he had not actually been told. He knew about rivers, and he could see how the land lay. She herself did not, but even she could see it now it had been pointed out to her. As for poor drowned Mr. Wetherby, he had fallen into the river while fishing, and he had been an old man—old Wetherby, the woman had called him—and there was nothing there to make her moment of horror about him seem any more reasonable. Helen thought it was not so much the fact of his death that had horrified her as the fact that Mr. Summers had told them of it, or perhaps even the way he had told them. She could not make out why this should be so, but then there was so much she could not make out about Mr. Summers. But above all, the woman herself had been an unlooked-for asset in the whole balance of advantage. She was as small and dark and resolute as Helen herself was tall and fair, and not, despite her spectacular good looks, really very good at looking after herself. She wondered what the woman and Steve would make of each other. She suspected that they would not like each other much, and this was another reason for not mentioning her. When she and Steve moved into Spandles, they would all meet, and then they could sort each other out. In the meantime she was very glad the woman was there, but for the moment she was keeping her to herself.

It was not until next day, when they were back in London, that she found that Steve had been keeping something to himself too. Not, in his case, a person's existence, but a person's non-existence. They had been talking about Ladon, and he said suddenly, "Oh by the way—you were right about Mr. Summers. He hasn't got a wife."

The casualness of it was so elaborate that she knew at once that he had at some point, presumably the day before, thought of telling her and deliberately decided not to. She was far more interested in this than she was in the fact itself. The fact itself meant little to her, because she had assumed as a matter of course that it was so. Why Steve should make such heavy weather of it she could not imagine, unless it was simply her own declared certainty on the point and the explanation she had given of it.

She said, "Oh? Where did you get that from?"

"The chap at the pub. I forget how it came up. I got the impression it's considered odd, because there have been Summerses at Calton since Domesday or something, and if he doesn't bestir himself, he'll be the last of the line. He was the only son, apparently."

She nodded. She was not going to say, "I told you so." She had indeed told him so, but she was not going to repeat the offence, if it was an offence. She said, "Oh well, he's still got time, surely. He's not all that old," and then wondered whether her casualness sounded as contrived to him as his had to her. She thought for a moment that he was going to remind her of her insistence that Mr. Summers was not the marrying sort, but if he was, he thought better of it. She wondered, not for the first time, what there was about Mr. Summers that provoked all this disingenuity among his acquaintances. Even the woman in the churchyard had seemed interested, almost surprised, that she had met him, but had then offered no comment on it whatever.

Steve said, "Oh certainly. I don't see him as a village Romeo exactly, but he's the sort of chap who might marry his housekeeper, don't you think?"

She did not think so, but was not going to rise to that either. She said, "Always provided he's got one," but she said it in a tone of cheerful inconsequence, as if the thing was of

no particular interest to her. She did not in fact believe in
the housekeeper any more than she had in a wife, but what
interested her was not the fact itself, but the strength and
immediacy of her conviction that Mr. Summers had no
women in his house, whatever he had abroad. He was not in
any way subject to women. That was what she had been trying to tell herself about him, ever since he had bowed himself off their threshold and gone off down the garden to the
fields along the river. He was not subject to women, and
nearly all the men she met were. They buzzed or drooled ac-
cording to their temperament, but they could none of them
help themselves. Mr. Summers had looked at her as the
others looked at her, but he had not buzzed or drooled. He
had behaved exactly as if she was a man, but he had not
looked at her like that. Steve did not mind the buzzers and
droolers. If anything, he was rather proud of them. Perhaps
that was why he was so curiously waspish about Mr. Summers. Surely he was not going to start being jealous, and of
Mr. Summers of all people, dark and oddly stately and hop-
pole high? That would be a very strange development indeed, but she knew, even as she thought how strange it
would be, that she would not altogether dislike it.

Steve wrote historical novels. Not, he was quick to explain, historical romances, of the kind that made so much
money for so many women writers, but novels set, and correctly set, in a historical period. Whatever he said about his
books, his readers did not seem to notice the difference, and
his readers were nearly all women. He had taken a degree in
history, but it had not in fact been a very good degree, and
he had not let his scholarship, such as it was, interfere with
his work. Helen might have had a difficult time with his
books, but she had said from the start that she was not his-
torically minded, and he had accepted that, perhaps even
welcomed it, and did not expect her to read all the books,
still less talk to him about them. He had not married her for
that. All the same, she had to be careful, especially in com-

pany. She knew too well what some of the people were thinking, especially the men, but she must not let her knowledge show. With the women it was easy, because although they all adored Steve, they mostly saw that they could not, merely as women, hold a candle to her, and she could afford to be nice to them, just as Steve could afford to be nice to the men who buzzed and drooled round her. It was a curious sort of mutual admiration society conducted at one remove. Up to now she had not let it worry her, but she was beginning to see that it might not always be without its difficulties.

Above all, she was doubtful whether it would work at all in a place like Ladon. It was Steve who had wanted to move to the country, and she had been glad of the change in principle, whatever doubts she now had about Ladon as a choice. But she wondered whether Steve would not before very long want to be back in London again, and what she would do if he did. Spandles was no week-end cottage. They were moving into it lock, stock, and barrel, and giving up the London flat altogether—partly at least, she suspected, because that was Steve's idea of what a successful author ought to do. But she thought he was not going to feel like a successful author half as much at Ladon as he did in London, and if his natural egotism was going to be thwarted by his super-ego, it might all get very uncomfortable. On the other hand, she supposed he might just start dashing up to London to see his agent, or to lunch with his publisher, or to attend one of the literary covens he patronised, and leaving her behind at Spandles, and she thought on the whole she would like that. Spandles was going to be lovely when she had finished with it, and in limited doses she could enjoy the brooding, skyey peace of the place much more on her own than with Steve being the successful author upstairs. It had been Steve's idea rather than hers that they should leave London, but she knew it would never be her idea that they should go back to it.

Meanwhile things were moving very quickly. Steve had money and he had a way with him, and when he wanted anything, he got it fast. It was, of course, true that the things he wanted, or at least admitted he wanted, were always within his practical power of achievement. Like many intensely egotistical men, he had a keen instinct for his own limitations. It remained an instinct, never explicitly stated, probably not even to himself, but it governed his actions effectively, and did much to guarantee their success. What would happen if he came up against something that he could neither get nor pretend convincingly that he did not want, Helen did not know. It had never to her knowledge happened since she had known him. She thought there was a real possibility that it might happen at Ladon, but it was a possibility that would not have occurred to him. He had not, as she had, been brought up in the country, and for all his love of rivers, he remained essentially a townsman. He was used to picking his way through the loose and heterogeneous society of town, taking what he wanted and could handle and leaving the rest, and the essentially homogeneous solidity of a village like Ladon would be something he had not reckoned with. When he did discover it, the danger was that he would try to make all the running, forcing his well-tried power to charm on everyone instead of letting the village make up its mind about him. And the power, practised as it was, had always up to now been used far more selectively than he would allow himself to admit. He had sowed his seed systematically on good ground, and the stony places would matter much more in Ladon than they ever had in town. She herself could handle Ladon if she had to, because she knew how to play a waiting game. But if she was accepted and he was not, and still more if he found himself accepted for her sake, it would be a complete reversal of their established roles, and he would not like it at all.

Meanwhile he continued to make all the running, and there was nothing she could do about it except go along with it and make the best of it. The lease of the flat was sold, and sold far better than she had expected. The formalities of Spandles were settled and plans made for the move. At least they would have far more room in the house than they had had in the flat, and there was no problem of what to leave behind. Everything could go, and even at this stage there were extras to be decided on and bought. Before they had been back in London a week he had fixed on the beginning of September for the move, and on the first of September to Spandles they went.

Chapter 4

———◆———

Helen recognised the voice as soon as she heard it, perhaps because she had been, consciously or unconsciously, hoping to hear it again. It called, "Anyone at home?" from downstairs in the hall, and Helen came out of one of the upstairs rooms with a bundle of stuff in her arms, and dumped it unceremoniously on the floor of the landing and hurried down the stairs. The front door stood wide open, as she had left it deliberately, with the mild September sunshine and the sweet, scentless air coming in through it, but indivisibly, as if you could feel the light moving or the air was coloured. The expected woman, the woman in the churchyard, stood just inside the doorway, looking up at her as she came down the stairs.

Helen said, "Oh hullo. How nice of you to come," and they smiled at each other.

"Well," the woman said, "we had a rather hurried conversation when you were here last, and it seemed only polite to come and call now that you've really arrived. My name's Fearon, by the way, Celia Fearon. My husband's Charles. We live in the village."

"Anderson," said Helen. "I'm Helen, and my husband's Steve. Well, Stephen professionally, but ordinarily Steve."

Mrs. Fearon said, "Oh we know who you are. I mean, we know your husband's Stephen Anderson, and that he writes, and what he writes. You're the surprise. We hadn't expected anything half so beautiful. Charles is longing to see you."

There was something in the way she said it, but Helen
could not quite make out what, some underlying assumption
that Celia Fearon took for granted but that she could not be
expected to know. Helen said, "Oh well, I hope he won't be
disappointed," but it was merely something to say, and she
looked at the vivid, pale face a little anxiously, needing an
explanation.

Celia Fearon saw the anxiety and came to her rescue. She
said, "Oh sorry. I thought you'd have been told. One always
assumes everyone knows everything. Charles is crippled. He
can't get out much. You'll have to come and see him." She
said it in a perfectly matter-of-fact way, neither apologising
for it nor seeking sympathy.

Instinctively, Helen took her tone from hers. An expression of sympathy was unavoidable, but she kept it almost to
a formality. "I'm so sorry," she said. "No, we hadn't heard.
We haven't seen many people yet. What's the trouble?"

"Nothing organic. An accident, years back, soon after we
were married. He's astonishingly cheerful about it, but of
course it makes difficulties. He lacks company a bit. I suppose we both do. That's why he was so delighted when I
told him about you."

Helen could not have said, afterwards, whether she had
actually heard something upstairs or whether she had
merely remembered Steve and assumed what he would do,
but she knew suddenly that he was listening from the upstairs landing. He had chosen the front room on the left,
looking south and east, as his working room, and he had
been busy there, setting up the sectional book-shelves and
unpacking his books as he went along, when she had hurried
down from the bedroom on the other side. He would not be
consciously eavesdropping. He was waiting for the moment
to come downstairs and meet the visitor—not exactly make
an entrance, but come downstairs when the moment seemed
ripe, though why one moment should seem riper than another he probably could not have said and certainly would

not consciously calculate. All the same, it irked her to have
him there, especially when it occurred to her that she had
still not mentioned to him her earlier meeting with Celia
Fearon. She was determined to have this out now, in Mrs.
Fearon's presence, and so save later explanations in private,
or at least in some way defuse them. She said, "Look, you
must meet Steve. Hold on a moment." She went back up a
couple of stairs and called, "Steve!" up the staircase. "Steve!
Do come. We've got a visitor." It was a small, harmless, quite
deliberate piece of play-acting. At least, she hoped it was
harmless. It was for Celia Fearon's benefit rather than
Steve's, but even as she did it, she knew that she would not
be an easy audience to play to. At least she could trust Steve
to play his part, and he did. There was a pause of exactly
the right duration, and then footsteps on the landing, and
Steve appeared at the head of the stairs. If necessary he
would have tip-toed back into his room and come out of it
again, but she doubted if he had judged it necessary. He
stood for a moment at the top of the stairs looking down at
them. Then he smiled his nicest smile at Celia over her head
and started coming downstairs. She knew that smile so well.

She said, "Steve, this is Mrs. Fearon. She lives in the village. She and I met for a moment when we were there last
month, and now she has come to visit us."

He said, "How very nice," and went past her and took
Celia's hand in his. She knew that hand-clasp, too. Once,
only once, when they had first met, he had done it to her,
and she had seen him do it dozens of times since to other
people. She knew how effective it was. There was warmth in
it, and just a touch of almost boyish impulsiveness. She did
not mind his doing it to Celia, but she could not help wondering how she would take it, not whether she would take it
too seriously, but whether she would not take it seriously
enough. She had anticipated trouble between these two, but
now that they had met, the possibility worried her. There

was still nothing she could do about it, or not when they were both there.

Celia had got her hand away now. Helen, naturally, had never shaken hands with her, but she knew her hand would be cool and a little hard and non-committal, like the rest of her. Not that she was a person who would refuse in all circumstances to commit herself. She must, God knows, have committed herself to her husband these many years in a way that Helen shrank from the mere thought of. But she was not going to be pushed into the slightest degree of self-committal against her will, still less cajoled into it by a warm smile and an impulsive hand-clasp. And unless Helen was mistaken, she would have done her home-work. She would have read the books, or some of them, and Helen found it impossible to believe that she would have liked them. Steve almost certainly did not know what he was up against. Nevertheless, he was doing his best. He said, "And how long have you been in this delectable place?"

Celia stood back, smiling at him pleasantly, and just for a moment moving her eyes to include Helen in the smile. She said, "Oh a long time now. I hope you find it delectable. It has its points, and it suits us well enough, but it's not to everyone's taste."

It was the hope Steve would not like. She should have said she was glad he found the place delectable, not she hoped he would, because he had already, by merely using the word, implied that he did, and to say that she hoped he would threw doubt on his judgement—or its validity, at least, or even more dangerously on its honesty. And delectable was a silly word at best. It was one of Steve's words, not in his books but in his conversation, but in Celia's mouth it was too clearly a quotation. You could tell by the way she said it that she would never use it herself.

As she knew he would, Steve saw the challenge at once. He always did. He never anticipated a challenge, at least not from a woman, but he saw it at once if it was there. He smiled at Celia more warmly than ever. He said, "Oh I shall. I already do. Helen's the one who still needs to be persuaded. A bit, anyhow. I hope you'll help to persuade her." He reached out a hand and laid it on Helen's arm, and drew her slightly towards him, as if to emphasise how important her agreement was to him, and dare this cool, smiling woman to treat them as anything but a couple. It was very deftly done. Even Celia must recognise its deftness. Whether she would believe it was another matter, and Helen could not make up her mind whether she wanted her to or not.

Celia said, "I shouldn't think of trying to persuade her." She said it perfectly pleasantly, but it was quite uncompromising. Cajoling was as foreign to her as it was natural to Steve. Then she smiled at Helen. "I certainly hope you'll stay," she said. "We need some new faces. But it's for you to decide."

It was not, of course, for Helen to decide. If it had been, they almost certainly would not have come. She knew it, and Steve knew it. Helen thought very probably Celia already knew it too. Once more, she could not make up her mind whether to be glad of this or not. She was immediately and enormously glad of Celia, but she was going to be a considerable complication in Helen's own relations with Steve, and she was not sure where the balance lay. They were faced already with the difference between life in a village and life in London. In London Steve would have skirted round Celia, but there could be no skirting round her here. They were all in it together, and would have to find a way of getting on. She hoped he would get on with Charles, but Charles was still an unknown quantity, and it was not generally the men he got on with. She said, "Well, we're here for a year anyway. Let's give it a run," but she said it in her most casual, dismissive sort of way, and at once changed the subject. She said to Steve, "Mrs. Fearon's got an invalid husband, who can't get out much. So it'll be for us to go and visit them." She turned to Celia. "If we may," she said.

Steve said, "Good Lord, that's bad. I'm sorry." He was, too. He hated sick people. Helen herself had never been ill since they were married, and she did not know what would happen if she was. He said, "Shouldn't we be a burden to you?" He was looking for an honourable way out, but Celia would have none of it.

"Not a bit," she said cheerfully. "Charles would love to see you. He's perfectly fit, only he can't move much, and of course he gets bored. You must come and dine with us when you've got straightened out and aren't too busy."

Helen said, "Any time. We'd love it. You fix a day and let us know."

"That would be marvellous," said Steve, "if you're certain we shan't be a nuisance." He was clearly to some extent re-assured by Celia's account of her husband, but was still keeping something in reserve.

Celia said, "Well, come on Thursday. There'll only be the four of us. Not a reception committee. You can meet other people in your own time."

Steve said, "Other people being what?" He said it in a light-handed, gossipy sort of way, but he really wanted to know. There was even, to Helen's accustomed ear, a touch of apprehension in it. She thought he was just beginning to see the difficulties she had seen from the start.

"Well," said Celia, "not much, and that's a fact. We've got a doctor, a good one. At least, he's excellent with Charles. We haven't got a parson. I mean, we have, but we share him, and he lives five miles away. Not a proper Agatha Christie cast at all. We haven't got a colonel who can pat your wife's arm and call her m'dear, and we haven't got an attractive widow with a past who can entangle you in her present."

"Pity about the widow," Steve said. "I can do without the colonel. Haven't we got a squire?"

She shook her head. "Not really, no. We're not really feudal at all. It's a very small parish, you know. There's only the one big farmer."

Helen said, "Mr. Summers?"

"Matthew Summers, that's right."

"Matthew," said Steve. He said it almost gleefully. "Matthew Summers. It's a marvellous name for a farmer. Pure seventeenth-century. But he wouldn't be a squire?"

He was still enjoying his private joke, but Celia answered him perfectly seriously. "Not a squire," she said, "no. No social overtones. But the fount of authority by prescriptive right. King rather than squire. And there is a Republican party."

Steve said, "I can hardly wait," and Celia looked at him steadily. Helen knew that look, because she had caught herself once or twice looking at Steve in exactly the same way, with that same touch of incredulity, as if he could not be quite real.

Finally Celia said, "Well, you have met him, haven't you? Matthew Summers, I mean. I think you said he'd come to see you when you were last here."

Helen came in on this. It was partly that she did not want anything about her original conversation with Celia Fearon to be left unexplained. But there was something else, too, though it was only when she thought about it later that she identified it. She knew then that she had had an almost desperate urge to stop Steve's saying anything more about Mr. Summers, at least to Celia. She was not quite sure why. Partly at least it was the way Celia had been looking at him, but there had been more in it than that. She had had an instinctive apprehension that Steve was on dangerous ground and did not know it. It was like seeing a man cutting capers on a minefield. Not quite that, because it was not damage to the man himself that she was mainly afraid of. She said, "Yes indeed. He was very polite and helpful. But I was a bit puzzled by him, I must say. I couldn't place him, some-

how. He didn't seem like a farmer, but I couldn't think what
he did seem like. He's certainly an odd looker. But in a way
unexpectedly impressive. I'm most interested to hear what
you say about him. It fits, I think. Steve was told that he was
the last of a long line, but hadn't married."

Celia was looking at her now—not, she was thankful to
see, in the way she had been looking at Steve, but with interest and a sort of detachment, looking at her as it were
through narrowed lids, where up to then she had been all
wide-eyed friendliness. Her eyes, Helen decided suddenly,
were the most important thing about her. She had no great
claim to good looks, but the eyes held you. You had to
watch them all the time, even more than with most people,
to know where you were with her. Then Celia opened her
eyes wide again, or seemed to, and smiled at her. The smile
was friendly enough, but there was something in it that had
not been there before—a touch of amusement, perhaps. But
she was not sure whether she was amused at her, or at
Steve, or at the pair of them and the relation between them.
Celia said, "That's quite right. I've met it before in members
of old families, especially landholders. This sort of assumed
authority, I mean. I'm not sure whether it's inherited or
acquired. But it can be disconcerting, especially when the
appearance doesn't seem to go with it."

Steve said suddenly, "But this is pure *King Lear*. Do you
remember? 'Whom wouldst thou serve?—You.—Dost thou
know me, fellow?—No, but there is that in your face I
would fain call master.—What's that?—Authority.' But not
Matthew Summers, surely to God. I don't see him as King
Lear." He was pleased with his quotation, and looked from
one to the other of them, smiling.

It was Celia who was determined to de-fuse the thing
now. She laughed cheerfully. "Not quite King Lear," she
said, "no, I agree. Still, if you're going to live in Ladon,
you'll find it better to have him on your side. He can get
things done, you know?"

Steve was still cheerful, too. "Or I can join the Republican party," he said. "Helen can be a royalist if she likes. But I doubt if we'll come to blows over it." He smiled at Celia, all warmth again. "Look," he said, "if you'll excuse me, I must go and get on with my unpacking. I'm up against a deadline, and must have somewhere to work. Anyway, I look forward to Thursday." He sketched a gesture of farewell, half a wave and half a blessing, and turned and went back upstairs. He walked upstairs very well, and both the women watched him go.

It was Helen who turned first. She turned quickly, because she did not want to turn at the same time as Celia and meet her eyes as she did so. She did not want to meet her eyes because she was afraid of what she might see in them. It was only when she had got her face to the open door that she heard Celia say, "I must be going too. Charles will be wondering where I've got to. But he'll be pleased about Thursday." She stopped and turned, so that Helen had to stop and face her. But she need not have worried. There was nothing of what she had feared in the wide grey eyes, only a shadow of something that might almost be anxiety. She said, "You will come, won't you?"

"Oh we'll come all right," said Helen. "We'd neither of us miss it for the world. About half past seven?"

"That'll do fine." Celia was out of the door now, and had turned onto the path that led round the west side of the house to the yard at the back. She would have left a car there, of course, though Helen had not heard it come. "Don't bother to come any farther," she said. "I know you're busy, and I can find my own way out." She stopped for a moment. Then she said, "Helen—do you mind if I call you Helen?"

"Of course not."

She nodded. "Well Helen, then—don't let your husband get up against Matthew Summers if you can help it. There's no need to, and it wouldn't help."

Helen said, "I'll do my best, I promise you," and Celia nodded and turned and went off along the path. She had said "your husband," not "Steve." And Helen knew that her promised best would be of no real use. She sighed and went back into the hall and up the stairs.

Chapter 5

There was no denying that the house was unprepossessing, and Helen felt an unmistakable stab of disappointment. She knew it was unreasonable, and doubled her unreason by feeling that it was all her own fault, because she had not meant to come and knew she should not have. She was still given to these childish guilt reactions, but nowadays they were usually something to do with Steve. She knew they were childish, and as it were spat them out as quickly as she could, but not generally before she had caught the sour taste of them in her mouth. It was nonsense, of course. It was perhaps a little inconsiderate to call on such a household without warning, but she did not believe that if Celia was at home, she would be anything but glad to see her, and if she was not, she could simply go back to the car. But Helen had done her shopping in the village without seeing Celia anywhere, and she had wanted to find out where the Fearons lived before Thursday evening. As for the house, it was a plain brick box, rendered over like all the rest, with no garden, but a little rather untidy grass on one side of it and a garage on the other. And what else could she have expected with Celia tied down the way she must be?

In any case, Helen was committed now. She marched up the short flagged path with her shopping basket on her arm and stood in front of the door, looking for a bell-push, but coming to the conclusion that she was going to have to use the rather tarnished brass knocker. She heard the soft trun-

dling noise just before the voice, but the voice hailed her as
she turned towards it. It said,

"Was this the face that launched a thousand ships
And burned the topless towers of Ilium?"

It was beautifully pitched, but resonant and full of zest,
so that even before she actually got her eyes on the figure in
the wheel-chair, she knew there was nothing here to need
pity or delicate handling. His big square shoulders were a
little hunched, as if all the power of his body had gone into
them, and his thick grey hair was rather curiously clipped
round the head, so that she knew, as she might have known
if she had thought, that it was Celia who did the clipping.
Charles Fearon said, "Mrs. Anderson, I presume?" The skin
of his face was very healthy but unweathered and the eyes a
startlingly bright blue. He was enormously likable.

She said, "That's right. But no ships, I'm afraid."

"No?" he said. "It's a decadent age we live in. But golly,
I'd have pushed the boat out myself for a face like yours,
that's if I'd been fifteen years younger, and had the use of
my legs, and not been married to Celia. You're very beautiful, Mrs. Anderson." He looked at her as a woman likes to be
looked at, but neither buzzed nor drooled. And that, she
thought, makes two of them in Ladon, which was more than
she could reasonably have hoped for.

She said, "I hope I'm not being a nuisance. But I was
shopping in the village, and thought I might as well find out
where you lived. Is Celia in?"

"No," he said, "but she shouldn't be long. She had to take
the car to the garage. But never a nuisance. If you're not in
a hurry, come and talk to me till she comes." He spun the
chair round and set off the way he had come, and Helen
simply turned and walked after him. He turned the corner
of the house, and by the time she came to it he was on the
point of turning the far corner and disappearing round the
back. She did not know how long he could keep it up, but

over a short distance at least she would have to trot to keep
up with him. She turned the second corner and found herself
on a small grass-plot between the back wall of the house and
a thick screen of shrubs and half-grown trees. It was overlooked by nothing but the upstairs windows of the house itself. The back door of the house opened directly onto it,
with a low-pitched concrete ramp for the wheel-chair to go
in and out. There was a plain wooden table in the middle of
the grass with books and newspapers on it, and also, she noticed, a couple of folded ordnance survey sheets. There was
a single garden chair of canvas on a folding wooden frame.
Charles Fearon was already on the far side of the table as
she came round the corner, and he pointed to the chair. "Sit
down," he said. "It's Celia's chair, but there's another one in
the house. I spend a lot of time here when the weather's
right. It's as private as being in the house. There's not much
to see, of course, but then there's not much to see round
here wherever you are. It's not a country for views."

Helen said, "You can't even see the river." She had not
said it before, certainly not to Steve, but it must have been
in her mind, and now it just came out. She would not mind
what she said to Charles Fearon.

He looked at her. She had been afraid he would think it a
nonsensical thing to say, but he did not seem to. He was
perfectly serious. "Not even from Spandles?" he said.

She shook her head. "Not even from upstairs," she said.

"Ah," he said. "I've never been to the house, of course. I
mean, I've seen it from the road, but I was just carted
straight past. I really only know it on the map, but the contours are so damned flat you can't tell. I should have
thought being as near as that—"

Helen shook her head again. "It keeps itself hidden," she
said. She was sitting in the chair now with her basket on the
grass beside her, and he had moved his chair a little to face
her directly across the table.

He looked at her a moment in silence and then nodded. "You don't like it?" he said.

"Not awfully, no."

"Then why choose Spandles?"

"Steve likes it," she said. "The river, I mean. And I've got nothing really against it. I just don't fancy it. But I couldn't say why."

"No," he said, "no. But you may be right at that. I've not seen it myself, but I fancy it's quite dangerous in a quiet sort of way. Floods and so on. And it managed to drown old Wetherby, even without a flood."

"Yes," she said. "Was that in your time?"

"Just. But we hadn't been here long, and weren't really in touch yet. I've heard people talk of it since, of course. No one seems to be very clear how it happened. But then he was getting on a bit, and he was a fisherman, and any fisherman will risk his neck for something that would hardly make him a decent breakfast. You don't fish?"

"Not me," she said. "Steve does." He did, too, or said he did. She had never known him do it, but he had all the tackle, and liked to talk of himself as a fisherman. At some time, before she had known him, he had been a climber, or said he had. That, too, would be a thing he saw himself as, but he had long since given it up, and for all she knew he might in fact have given up fishing as well. Only here he had the river, and she did not know what he would do.

Charles nodded. "Well, you tell him to be careful," he said. People were always telling her what to tell Steve. It was no good explaining. He said, "They say the banks are very steep and undercut in places, and just clay anyway. It's difficult to get out once you're in, that's the thing. And the water's deeper than you'd expect, and full of weed. Once you're in you can't get out, and once you go down you don't come up. Anyway, that's what they say. I've never even seen the damned thing. As you say, it keeps itself hidden—at any rate, from the likes of me." He smiled at her suddenly. "Not that that worries me. There are a lot of things I'd like to see, but the River Lod is well down my list of priorities." He had stopped looking at her and was looking at his hands as they lay in his lap. She could not see his legs. They were bundled up in a rug. He was still smiling, but talking quietly, almost to himself. Then he raised his eyes to hers, and his face was serious again. He said, "But you're fully mobile, and you live near it. If you don't like it, keep away from it. The very fact that you don't like it wouldn't help if you did get in. You'd be apt to feel the river was against you. You're young and strong, and I expect you're a good swimmer, and all that you'd need in fact would be to keep your head. But I shouldn't say you're extra good at keeping your head, and being afraid of the river would make it worse." He smiled at her again. "And you're much too beautiful to drown," he said.

She found her mouth suddenly dry, and realised that it was a little open and that she was breathing through it as she stared at him. She shut it and moistened her lips with her tongue. She felt suddenly enormously young and defenceless, but she made herself smile. "I'm sorry," she said. "Does it show all that much? About losing my head, I mean."

His head went up with a jerk, and for a moment he looked almost angry, but not with her. "Good God," he said, "you mustn't take anything I say seriously. I talk too much. It's a way of—well, you can understand. I didn't mean you're a flibberty-gibbet. You're much nicer than one could reasonably expect with those looks. But I doubt if they give you the confidence they ought to. You don't know your own strength, my girl, and that's a fact." He was quiet for a moment, still looking at her. Then he said, "I haven't met your husband, of course."

The connection was clearly there in his own mind, so that his last sentence was in some way a gloss on what he had said before, but she was not sure how she was supposed to take it. She was not even sure she particularly wanted to know. Her relation with Steve was something she had always, as it were, played by ear, and she had never encouraged anyone to examine it any more closely than she did herself. Now she had Celia, whose thinking she fancied she understood, but who said nothing, and Charles, who said everything, but whose thinking she could not altogether follow. Between them, they looked like they were forcing her to come to an understanding of her own position, and this was a thing she instinctively shrank from. As she often did, she fell back on words that followed the conversation with reasonable coherence, but had the effect of diverting it to safer ground. She said, "No; well, you'll be meeting him on Thursday. I know he's looking forward to it."

"Good," he said. "Me too." But she wondered as he said it whether Charles Fearon was in fact looking forward to meeting Steve any more than she suspected Steve was looking forward to meeting him. Above all, she wondered what advance reports he had had from Celia, if indeed he had had any. Celia was very good at not saying things, and Helen did not know how much or how little Celia had said to Charles. He said, "And you've met Matthew Summers?"

That at least must be something Celia had told him. She said, "Not since we moved in. But he came and met us when we were down here seeing the place." She was not saying anything more for the moment herself. Charles had raised the subject of Mr. Summers, and it was for him to pursue it if he wanted to. She very much hoped he would, but she was not going to do any prompting.

"An interesting character," he said.

"So I understood from Celia." She was still not offering anything of her own, but he looked at her with a small, half-teasing smile, so that she wondered whether she had made her determination too obvious.

Then he nodded. He said, "And what account did Celia give of him?"

She found this difficult. Surely he knew Celia's view of Mr. Summers, and if he did, he would be asking for her version of it only to see what light it threw on her own. His interest had not changed, only his line of approach. If he did not know Celia's view, or thought he did not, it suggested that on this, too, Celia had not been talking, and to Charles. Once more, she did not know what Celia had said to him, and did not want to tell him more than Celia had chosen to tell her. But this must be nonsense. Celia had talked freely to her and Steve. There was nothing confidential about it. The idea that she would not want it repeated to Charles was absurd. It was still her reaction to Mr. Summers that he was for some reason interested in, and that for some reason, perhaps because she was uncertain of it herself, she did not particularly want to talk about. The only thing was to answer his question as asked and let him make what he liked of it. She said, "Oh I think she was talking about people in the village generally. Yes, that's right. She had asked us to dine with you on Thursday, and then she said it would be just the four of us, and we could meet other people later. And then Steve asked what other people there were, and that ultimately led to Mr. Summers. I think she said he had great influence in the village, though there was a faction opposed to him. A Republican party, she called it. Steve is inclined to think Mr. Summers a bit of a joke, and rather questioned his influence, but she insisted that he had this sort of inherited authority, and that we'd do better to have him on our side than against us."

He had been listening to her intently, his head slightly bowed and his eyes on his hands again. For a moment he stayed like that, and then he lifted his head and looked at her, and she was puzzled by the expression on his face. Above all, it was serious. For whatever reason he had asked the question, there was something here that really con-

cerned him. But there was also a hint of mockery in the blue
eyes, and she remembered having the same feeling with
Celia. As with Celia, she did not feel that the mockery was
primarily against herself, but there was irony somewhere.
Only she did not know whether the irony was the same for
Charles as for Celia, and she felt suddenly uneasy. She was
in the same minefield as Steve had been in. She was not
capering as he had capered, but even for a person walking
sedately the mines were still there. He said, "A Republican
party. I like that." He was smiling now, but she was still not
altogether easy with the smile. "That's Celia's phrase, all
right. Matthew Summers being king, I take it?"

She smiled into his smile, and spoke as lightly as she could
and more lightly than for some reason she felt. "Well, more
or less," she said. "Steve asked if Mr. Summers was squire,
and she said not squire, because there were no social implications, but he had a sort of inherited authority as the last of
a long line of landholders, a sort of uncrowned king. It was
then she said there was a Republican party, and I remember
later Steve threatened to join it, but of course the whole
thing wasn't serious."

He nodded, still smiling, and then his head went up with
a jerk, and they both heard the car pull into the garage at
the side of the house. "Here she is," he said.

They sat there waiting for Celia to appear and saying
nothing more to each other. The back door was open, and
they could hear her moving about inside the house, opening
and shutting cupboards and drawers, as if she were putting
shopping away. Then there were footsteps in the passage
and she came out of the door, and the two faces turned towards her as she came. There had been a curious constraint
in those few moments of waiting, and Helen was glad they
were over. Charles said, "Your beautiful friend came to see
you, and I persuaded her to stop and talk to me till you got
back."

Celia smiled at him and then at Helen. If she was sur-

prised to find her there, she did not show it. She said to
Helen, "I'm so glad. I wondered whether you might have. I
saw your car in the village street, but couldn't see you anywhere."

Helen said, "Well, I didn't see you anywhere and hoped
you'd be at home, but your husband said you'd gone to the
garage."

Charles said, "What's all this husbandry? I'm Charles,
and Celia's Celia, and you're Helen, and Steve's Steve, or
will be when we meet. Let us by all means respect matri-
mony, but not bandy it about." He turned to Celia. "Well,"
he said, "how's Jack Winthrop and his pretty Joan? And
what does he say about the car?"

Celia said, "Half a minute while I get a chair." She went
into the house and came back with another folding chair,
which she put down between Helen and Charles. Then she
said, "It wants a new carburetor—well, not the whole carburetor, but one of its vitals. He hasn't got it, but will get it in
a day or two. He says that will get the petrol consumption
back to normal."

Charles said, "Well, thank God for that." He turned to
Helen. "You haven't met Jack yet—Jack Winthrop at the garage?"

"I don't think so. I've been there for petrol, but it was a
boy at the pumps. He couldn't have been the boss man."

"No, that's Ernie. There's no mistaking Jack. A bit fierce
and intellectual, but a marvellous mechanic and almost
painfully honest with his ignorant public. One of our leading Republicans."

"And he's got a pretty wife?"

"That's right, Joan. Not intellectual at all, but very taking.
Perhaps that's what makes Jack so fierce."

Helen said, "I'll be meeting them, I expect. Look, I really
must be getting on." She turned to Celia. "I'm sorry to go
just when you get back," she said, "but we'll see you on
Thursday."

Celia was looking at Charles with a curious intensity. Her face was as nearly as possible expressionless. There was nothing to show what she was thinking, only this unmistakable concentration of thought. Then she turned to Helen and smiled. "Of course," she said. The two women got up, and Helen said good-bye to Charles, and they went into the house and left him sitting there.

When they got to the front door, Helen said, "Till Thursday, then," and Celia said, "Yes, good," and Helen went off down the path to the gate. Something was worrying her. She was not sure what, but it might come to her later. For the moment she must get back to Spandles and Steve.

Chapter 6

When she got out of bed and went to the window, she found the mist back on the fields, as it had been the first day they had driven to the village. It lay in a white level sheet as far as she could see in any direction from the front of the house. The house itself and the garden stood above it, with the mist lapping the top of the garden steps, but beyond the garden there was nothing high enough to get its head out of it—not a tree, nor a fence, nor a building, nor a living creature. The white vapour could not be more than seven or eight feet deep, but it covered everything. She did not know how long it would last. Not long, probably, once the sun got well above it, but that would not be for some time yet. It was still not yet seven. The sun was up, but low and red and itself shrouded in vapours. Its light was reflected down from the white sky overhead onto the white mist below, but it had no radiant heat yet to penetrate and dissolve the mist. There was no heat of any sort. The air was chill and fresh and smelt of nothing. The mist had no smell of its own, as a sea-mist has.

She shivered, and gathered up an armful of clothes and went along to the bathroom, shutting the bedroom door quietly behind her. Steve was still asleep and would be for some time yet. He had worked late, so late that she did not know when he had come to bed. He often did when he was pressed for time with a book, and he was pressed now, because the move and the business of settling in had made a big hole in the time he had allowed himself. He wrote easily, or seemed to, but he wrote very much as a matter of business routine, and set himself a strict timetable. There was nothing to be said against his writing at all, so long as you did not have to take the product too seriously. Even his businesslike methods were not to be held against him. There had been great writers, she knew, who had been equally businesslike, and his business at least was profitable. It was just that the books were not very good as books. She had never known, and supposed she would never know, how good he thought them himself, but it did not do for anyone else to question their quality. She pulled her nightdress over her head and ran hot water into the basin. She had a sense of urgency, but was not sure how far she simply wanted to get her clothes on again against the cold air and how far she wanted to have as much of the day as possible to herself before Steve woke up.

She got dressed and hung her nightdress on the hook on the bathroom door. She was not going back to the bedroom. She did her hair as well as she could in the bathroom mirror, but left her make-up till later. She came out of the bathroom quietly, stood for a moment listening, and then tip-toed down the stairs. The kitchen was warm and peaceful. She had left it in order last night, and it was still in order except for a cup and saucer and a small saucepan soaking in the sink, which meant that Steve had brewed himself a hot drink at some time of the night before he went up to bed. A clock ticked steadily on the shelf over the stove. It was not the same clock as they had had in the kitchen in her childhood, it probably did not even have the same sound, but the effect was exactly the same. It was the voice of the odd hours, of the late night and the very early morning, because it was only then you heard it. It ticked in the same way all day, but you did not notice it. She was filled with a sudden sense of adventure and excitement that came to her straight out of her childhood, because she had got the world to herself, and everyone else was asleep upstairs and did not even know where she was or what she was doing. She boiled a little water and made herself a cup of tea with a tea-bag in the bottom of a cup. It was not the way she would ever make tea as a rule, but it was exactly what she wanted now. She drank it quickly in wickedly hot gulps, leaning against the sink and gazing through the window into the white blank world outside.

She knew that as soon as she had drunk her tea, she was going out. She was in a hurry to drink it and get out, because once she was out, no one could tell, when she got back, how long she had been gone. That made time your own, whereas if they saw you go out, their time followed you, and you were never free of it. She finished her tea, threw the tea-bag into the waste-bin, and put the cup to soak in the sink beside Steve's. If he came down and saw it, it might tell him that she had gone out early, just as his had told her that he had to be late, but it still would not tell him when. She went, still quietly, into the back porch. This was the real entrance-hall of the house, as she had known from the start it would be, with coats and hats hanging on pegs, and boots and outdoor shoes lined up along the skirtings. She put on a light mackintosh, stepped into a pair of gumboots, and tied a headscarf over her hair. She thought of taking a stick, which she used when the going was likely to be rough, or when she was in a hurry, because she had an ankle that was not wholly dependable, but decided against it. She was in no hurry once she was out of the house. She opened the door quietly and went out into the yard.

Even here the air was misty and surprisingly cold. It was absolutely still. Nothing moved and nothing made any sound anywhere. For all her soft boots, she tip-toed across the yard, through the small gate, and along the path under the west wall of the house. She went down the front garden as if she were walking down a beach, with her eyes on the white sea in front of her, knowing she was going down into

it but still a little breathless at the thought of it. At the top
of the steps she hesitated a moment, but this would not do.
When Steve awoke, he would get up and go to the window,
because in the country that was what you always did, and
the window overlooked the front garden. At any moment his
voice might hail her from the window, and she would have
to go back. She opened the gate at the top of the steps, letting up the latch so gently that it made no click at all, and
went down the steps into the mist.

She had somehow expected to find herself in an invisible
world, where she would have to grope her way, but of
course it was not like that at all. She could see the grass at
her feet perfectly clearly, but only for a few paces in any direction. The light was quite bright but absolutely colourless.
It lit nothing but the mist and that small circle of grass
round her feet, which would move with her as she moved.
She walked a dozen yards and then turned and looked back.
She could no longer see the steps. The whole front of the
house was perfectly clear, but floating baseless above an indeterminate whiteness. She looked at the one window, but
there was no one there. Then she turned and went on, heading southwards across the fields. The next time she turned to
look back, only the top half of the house was visible. She
supposed if she went far enough, that too would vanish, and
then she would have nothing to get back on but her sense of
direction, which in this tiny, enclosed world she did not
trust an inch. Then she thought that sooner or later she must
come to a fence, and she could follow the fences, east and
west or north and south, and come back on the same line.
Not that it mattered. The mist would not hold forever, and
in the meanwhile her time was her own. She went on steadily, never turning to look behind. The fence, when she came
to it, was nothing but four strands of wire, with posts faintly
visible to left and right, and she was almost on it before she
saw it at all. She put her hands on the top wire and found it
beaded with hanging drops of water, which shook off as the

taut wire moved under her hands. Her headscarf and the front of her hair under it were beaded with moisture too, and when she touched it, the front of her mackintosh was damp. With a sudden access of childish, Boy Scout cunning, she took out her handkerchief and tied it to the top strand of wire. She had only to follow the fences, right and left as if they were streets, to get back to her handkerchief, and then, when she got back to it, strike out at right angles to the line of the fence, and then before long she must see the house again. She did not really believe she would have to do this, but in the meantime the thought pleased her. She knotted one corner of the handkerchief to the wire, leaving the rest hanging, very white and visible in the white light. Then she turned right-handed and set off along the fence.

She went faster now, and when she came to the cross-fence running north and south, she dodged through the wire and followed it left-handed, heading south again. She did not tell herself she was making for the river, but if she went south far enough, there was only the river to come to. She came to another east–west fence and thought of turning left-handed along it, to get back onto her original line, but this would only complicate matters. If she kept on down her present line, and the mist still held, all she would have to do would be to come back up it and take, as it were, the second turning right until she found her handkerchief. Second, at least, so far. If she crossed another east–west fence, of course, third. She did not know how many east–west fences there were between the house and the river. For the moment she ducked through this one and followed her own fence southwards. She saw nothing all the way but the fence ahead of her and the circle of dark grass round her feet and the white mist shutting it all in. She heard nothing but the rustle of her mackintosh and the swish of her boots in the grass. She crossed two more fences, counting them carefully in her head. She had no idea how far she had come or how long she had been walking, but time and distance seemed

unimportant. It was only when she came to the fifth
east–west fence that she realised the mist was getting
thicker. Her visible world was so small now that she had to
check herself suddenly to avoid the cross-wires, and when
she looked right and left, she could not see the posts that
held them. She went through them, went on a few yards,
and then stopped and listened. It had occurred to her that
the mist would be thicker over the river, and in any case she
must surely be getting close to it now. She stood there in the
total silence straining her ears for sounds of water, but
wherever the Lod was, it ran silent under its steep bank and
did nothing to betray its presence.

She went on again, but slower. She was not sure what
would happen to her fence when it came to the bank, or
whether the bank itself would be guarded by a final cross-
fence. Surely if the banks were as dangerous as Charles
Fearon had said they were, they would be fenced, or the
cattle would be at perpetual risk. Or perhaps the last fence
was well back from the bank, and was the one she had already passed. She had not left it very far behind. Then a
taller, more solid post loomed out of the mist ahead, and as
she came to it, she saw simultaneously that there was no
wire beyond it, and that a yard, no more, ahead of her the
grass stopped too. That was all there was to see. The dark
grass, which had circled her all the way from the house,
stopped short, and in front of her, above, below, and on either side, there was nothing now but the white mist. Under
the mist, almost under her feet, she knew there was dark
water creeping under its high bank, but she could not see or
hear it.

For a moment she stopped short, horrified by the stealthy
danger of it. Then curiosity, or whatever it was that had
brought her all this way, re-asserted itself, and she went forward a step at a time, holding tightly with her right hand
first the top strand of wire and then, when she came to it,
the post itself, and peering always downwards and forwards.

She could see the edge of the bank clearly now. It was grassed to the very lip and ended as sharply as if it had been cut off with a knife. She could still not see the water. She thought if she lay flat on the grass and peered over, she would be bound to see it, but she could not do that and retain her hold on the post, and she remembered what Charles Fearon had said about the banks being undercut. She imagined the turf giving way under her as she craned forward and shooting her head-first into the silent water, which was deep and full of weed, and where once you had gone down you did not come up again. That was enough to stop her. She had finished her exploration. She had come all the way to the river and still had not seen it, but she was ready now to take it on trust.

Then a fresh thought occurred to her, and she knelt where she was by the post, scrabbling among the west grass and the surface soil, feeling rather than looking for what she wanted. After a little scrabbling her fingers closed on a small pebble, hardly bigger than her thumb-nail and rounded like a pebble on a beach, but still hard stone. She got to her feet, transferred the pebble to her left hand, and then, still holding onto the post with her right, threw it forwards and downwards into the mist in front of her. The moment it had left her hand she checked the movement of her arm and froze there, with her left hand outstretched, listening. The sound was so long in coming that she thought she had imagined a river that was not there, but it did come. It was a tiny sound, blanketed by the mist and farther from her than she expected, but still unmistakable, the soft plop of a small hard thing falling into still water. The river was there and had taken her stone.

She began to back away from it, still holding onto the post with her right hand until she had backed past it, and had it between her and the river. Then she turned, and her hand, which had let go of the post, went up to her mouth, but not quick enough to stifle the scream that her lungs forced out of her. It was hardly a scream, not much more than a yelp, but very sharp in the total silence. Straight in front of her, blocking the line of the fence she had to follow home, an immensely tall figure loomed in the mist. She stood there, still with her hand to her mouth and the river at her back, and the figure began to come slowly towards her, moving in total silence. Then it said, "Good morning, Mrs. Anderson. The river is there, all right. There is no need to throw things at it."

She knew who it was, of course. She had known that even before she had heard the curiously deep voice and the deliberate speech. But still he came on, and she was still frightened of him. She would have been frightened of anyone coming towards her like that, with the unguarded bank behind her and the mist all round. She did not say anything. She just stood there, watching his face as it came out of the mist towards her and tilting her head farther and farther back as it got higher above her own. It was right over her now, looking down into hers, and smiling a little. The mere physical fear drained out of her, but she felt so weak that she thought her knees would buckle under her, and her mind was in a state of total confusion. She still said nothing, and his smile broadened and he said, "Don't worry. You're much too beautiful to drown," exactly as Charles Fearon had.

She said, "I don't want to drown." She said it in a small, choked voice, because her throat was dry and her head still tilted right back looking up at him. She sounded, even to herself, like a small girl saying she did not want to go to bed yet.

For a moment his face came very close to hers. The dark eyes were wide open, staring into her eyes, and the mouth was no longer smiling but drawn down with deep-cut lines at the corners. Then he drew a long breath and shook his head slowly, though whether at himself or at her she could not tell. "You shan't drown," he said, and his face lifted away from hers as he straightened up, and he stepped back a pace. Then he put out a hand to her. "Come on," he said, "I'll put you on your way home."

She was more in control of herself now. Even so, she felt no anger against him. She thought she ought to be angry, but could not see what there was to be angry about. She said, "Don't worry. I can find my way. I'll follow the wire."

He nodded. "Very well," he said. "The mist will clear soon, and your husband will be awake." He said it in a completely matter-of-fact tone, as if the two things were natural phenomena equally within his knowledge and somehow connected in his mind. "But you are on my ground here, and if you come onto my ground, you must expect to meet me."

She could not think what to say to this that would not involve her in complications of one sort or another. Finally she nodded and said, "All right," and he stood aside, and she went past him, walking along beside the wire towards the first of the cross-fences. For some extraordinary reason it suddenly occurred to her that he had not had his dark hat on, and in spite of herself she stopped and turned and looked back to make sure, but there was nothing behind her but the mist and the line of wire vanishing into it. She turned again and went on. She was hurrying now. She came to the first fence almost at once and ducked through it. It must, as she had thought, run quite close to the bank. All she had to do now was to turn right along the fourth fence and follow it until she found her handkerchief. It was as she turned right that the light changed quite suddenly from white to gold, and the edges of the world fell back, so that she saw the handkerchief while she was still quite a long way from it. It was limp and wet under her rather unsteady fingers as she untied it. She stuffed it into the pocket of her mackintosh. Then she turned to go northwards, and saw the top of the house almost at once.

She forced herself to walk slowly now. Her mind still hurried, but she did not want to be seen hurrying, and she needed to get her breath back. The house was in full sunlight as she came up the steps, and when she got onto the porch, she could hear Steve moving about in the kitchen. She stepped out of her boots and into her shoes, and took off her mackintosh and headscarf, and then the kitchen door opened and he was looking out at her. He said, "Hullo. I wondered where you'd got to." He had a cup and saucer in his hand.

"I went for a walk," she said. "I was awake, and it was a lovely morning. I hope I didn't disturb you."

"No, rather not. I haven't been awake long. I worked late. Like some tea?"

She said, "Oh yes please," and joined him in the warm kitchen. She knew simultaneously that she ought to mention her meeting with Mr. Summers, and that she would not mention it, and that no one else would, probably ever. Meanwhile there was the day to be getting on with, and she drank her tea quickly and went upstairs to finish her dressing. The mist had almost gone now, but even from upstairs you still could not see the river.

Chapter 7

She drove past the pumps and stopped in front of the garage doors, to show it was Jack she wanted, not Ernie. Ernie worked in the workshop as well, of course. There was not the trade to justify anyone whole-time on the pumps, even Ernie. He worked in the workshop, doing the routine stuff under Jack's supervision, but when it was only petrol, he came out in his overalls, wiping his hands on a bit of cotton waste. By the time Jack had finished with him, he would be a skilled mechanic, ready to earn very good money here or elsewhere, but for the moment he was not a consultant, merely a hand, and when she ignored the pumps and drove to the workshop door, it was Jack who came out, not Ernie. She knew it must be Jack here, but given the overalls she would have recognised him anywhere from Charles Fearon's description. A bit fierce and intellectual. He had the high, narrow, rather thrusting forehead that in her experience went more with a certain type of character than with great intelligence, and the hair brushed firmly back from it was disciplined for its length and unexpectedly grey for a man of that age. The face was disciplined, too, but slightly indignant, as if it anticipated injustice and was ready to challenge it. He looked like a Midlander.

He came out deliberately, looking at her all the way, and smiling slightly. So far as she knew, he had not seen her before, but he would recognise her from what he had heard, just as she recognised him. There was no question of his hanging back just to show he would not be put upon. He came as soon as he knew she was there. All the same, his whole approach ws calculated for effect. She thought almost everything he did would be calculated for effect, at least until people got to know him, because to him their attitude to him would be the most important thing about them, and he had to get it right from the start. He said, "Good morning, Mrs. Anderson. How can I help you?"

She was out of the car before he got to her, and found herself at least as tall as he was. Physically he was a slight man, but straight up and down, and very neat and efficient in his movements. He looked at her with great interest, but the interest was not quite of the kind she was used to. It was too detached. She had expected a certain degree of difficulty with him, but he did not seem difficult, only rather disconcerting, because of the quality of his interest and the way he smiled, as if he were enjoying some private joke. She said, "Good morning, Mr. Winthrop. I'm having trouble starting. It does start, but it takes a long time, and seems to be getting worse. Up to recently it was starting first go." Like most women, she called the car "it." Steve called any car "her," but then he did personalise things, just as he tended to depersonalise people. It was an ordinary saloon, fairly new and fairly good, because Steve could afford both, but ordinary.

Mr. Winthrop nodded, but said nothing, so that she felt bound to go on. She said, "I don't think it can be anything serious. But I'm afraid I don't know much about cars." She looked at him helplessly, not because she wanted to be the helpless little woman, but because she really felt helpless. She could have asked Steve, but he did not take her car very seriously. In any case, she did not think he would know. He took his own car very seriously, but she did not believe he knew much about that either.

To her relief, and perhaps a little to her surprise, Jack Winthrop took her statement simply at its face value. "No?" he said. "No, well, most of the people who drive cars don't, and you don't really need to, in fact, not with the modern car.

But you could learn a bit, you know, if you wanted to. There are plenty of books. And you might find it interesting."

She warmed to him suddenly, because he was being neither fierce nor intellectual, but treating her as an ordinary person. The fact that he treated her exactly as an equal pleased her rather than otherwise. One of our leading Republicans, Charles Fearon had said, but that had been nothing to do with social relations, only with Matthew Summers. Something nagged at her mind for a moment demanding attention, but then Jack Winthrop went on again, and she lost it. He said, "Well, anyhow, I'll have a look at her. You couldn't leave her here, could you? I'm on another job at the moment, and it's a bit urgent."

She had not thought of this, but was immediately anxious to accommodate him. She said, "Oh—well, I've got some shopping to do. I could come back, perhaps?" There was no reason in fact why she should not leave the car and walk home, and then ask Steve to bring her back later to collect it, only she did not think Steve would like that, either his having to drive her in or her walking home. She thought there was going to be enough difficulty between him and Jack Winthrop as it was, without getting him off on the wrong foot over this.

Jack shook his head, but he was still smiling. It was an almost indulgent smile now, as if it was not so much her suggestion that amused him as her accommodation. "Well," he said, "doesn't really give me much time, does it? But you don't want to have to carry your shopping home. I tell you what: You do your shopping and come back here. If I can have her ready for you, I will. If not, Joan will drive you back. That's my wife. She'll be wanting to meet you, and you'll have things in common. She'll be glad to run you back. But I'll have the car for you if I can. How's that?"

She said, "That's very kind of you." It was kind, too, only she was still not quite sure of the quality of his kindness. The wife would be Charles' pretty Joan, not bright but very

taking, who was perhaps responsible for her husband's fierceness. She had not found him fierce yet, but she wondered
what it was he expected her and Joan to have in common.
Perhaps just takingness and lack of intellect, a pair of dumb
blondes, if Joan was a blonde. She would see, anyhow.
Dumb or not, she did not really think Jack would have the
car ready when she got back from her shopping. She
thought that for some reason he wanted his wife to drive her
back. "All right," she said, "I'll go and do my shopping, and
see how you get on." She took her basket out of the car,
smiled at Jack, and set off along the road towards the shops.
Even before she was clear of the yard, she saw, out of the
corner of her eye, that he had gone back inside to his job.

He was still inside when she got back with her shopping.
Her car had been moved a few yards forwards, to clear the
garage doors, but she did not think anything else had been
done to it. There was a small saloon, which had not been
there before, standing on the other side of the yard, beyond
the pumps. The house on that side had a gate opening direct
onto the side of the yard, and would be where the
Winthrops lived. It was a newish house on one floor, a bungalow, not a cottage, very spruce and solid, but small. If
they had a family, they would be cramped for space, but she
did not think they had. She had not seen Joan yet, but Jack
did not feel like a family man, and the whole look of the
place was against it. No washing on the line, no toys in the
garden, no touch of the chaos that always seemed to her in-
separable from even well-behaved families. Ladon did not
go in for children much. She thought Celia would have liked
them, but she supposed they could not have them now, and
in any case she had her hands full with Charles.

She was so certain that her own car was not ready, and
that she would be driven home by Joan in the little saloon,
that she found herself making straight for it and the bungalow beyond it, but she knew this would not do. Instead, she
went to the workshop doorway. There was a big utility up

on a hoist, with Jack and Ernie under it, muttering to each other and peering up into its vitals. They did not see her so long as she stayed outside, but when she walked in and came between them and the daylight, Jack saw her and came towards her, ducking under the tail of the hanging car. Behind him, curiously top-lighted by a working lamp hung somewhere inside the oily metal-work, Ernie stared out at her, impassive and uncommitted, leaving her to the boss to handle. Jack said, "No luck yet, I'm afraid. But Joan'll run you back, if you'll go over to the house." He jerked his head in the direction of the bungalow. "She's expecting you. I'll bring yours back later, if that's all right for you."

She said, "But then how will you get back?" As she said it, it expressed kindly concern, but she knew, even as she said it, that she was really pointing up the complication of his arrangements. She still had the feeling that he could have sorted out her trouble in a few minutes without seriously interfering with his job on the big utility, but that for some reason he had preferred not to. But then she did not know anything about cars.

He smiled at her suddenly and broadly. She doubted whether he often smiled like that, and the smile did not sit easily on that narrow, essentially serious face. He said, "Fancy your thinking of that." She was not sure whether his surprise was at unexpected intelligence in a helpless blonde or unexpected consideration in the moneyed classes, but she did not think he guessed what had really made her say it. Intellectual or not, he was not really a very bright man. "Don't worry," he said. "Joan'll come along and run me back."

She noted Joan's universal availability, but did not comment on it. She would be seeing Joan anyhow. "All right," she said, "thank you. I'll go over and find her, shall I?"

"If you would," he said. They nodded to each other, Helen turned to walk across the yard, and Jack went back to the waiting Ernie. She wondered what would happen if she decided suddenly simply to go out of the yard onto the road and walk home. But she did not really want to carry her shopping, which was heavy, all the way home, and she was curious, now, to meet Joan Winthrop. In any case, she doubted whether she would be allowed to. Jack was back with Ernie under the hoist, and would not see her go, but unless she was mistaken Joan would be watching for her out of one of the side windows of the bungalow. She would have been told to.

She was not mistaken, because well before she got to the small saloon, let alone the side gate, the front door of the bungalow opened, and Joan Winthrop came out to meet her, so that they came up to the car almost simultaneously from opposite sides. She was not conscious of having formed any picture of her in her mind, but she found her appearance wholly unexpected. Above all, she was not a small woman. She was as tall as Helen herself, which meant that she was at least as tall as her husband, and she had delicate features, with curling brown hair and a warm, almost shy smile. There was absolutely no reason why she should not be and have all these things, but as pretty, dumb Joan, who helped to make her serious husband fierce, she did not seem to fill the bill. Perhaps it was merely Charles' way of talking. Charles had told her not to take anything he said seriously, and perhaps it was on this last point, which she had discounted as mere apology, that Charles was in fact mainly to be relied on.

Joan Winthrop said, "You'll be Mrs. Anderson, and Jack said I was to drive you home. Will that be all right?"

Helen said, "It's very kind of you. But really it wouldn't kill me to walk. Are you sure you can spare the time?"

"Oh I've got plenty of time." Consciously or not, she emphasised the "time" slightly, as if it were the thing she was most aware of and could most easily spare. "Will you get in this side?" she said. "Put your basket in the back."

Helen went round to the far side of the car and got herself installed. Joan Winthrop shut her in and went round and got into the driving seat. Helen said nothing because she was uncertain, now, what to say, but when she had got herself settled at the wheel Joan turned suddenly and smiled at her. "I was awfully pleased when Jack told me I had to drive you home," she said.

She was so disarming about it that Helen spoke almost without thinking. "When did he?" she said.

Joan had started the car now, and they were moving out onto the road. She kept her eyes ahead and took the question in her stride. "Oh as soon as you'd gone," she said. "He phoned through. There's a line from the garage. Didn't he tell you?"

"He told me you would if necessary, but he might have my car ready for me."

Joan laughed. It was only a small laugh, and she still did not turn her head or look at Helen. "Oh that's Jack all over," she said. It was impossible to tell what she meant, or even to judge the quality of her laughter, but Helen could not ask. Joan said, "He'll do yours presently, and you'll find it's all right. He's a wonder with cars."

"And he'll bring it back to Spandles, and you'll come along and drive him home?"

"Is that what he said?"

"That's what he said, yes."

"That's what it'll be, then. But you won't see him, not if he can help it. He'll just leave your car in the yard and be off. But you'll find it'll work all right."

Helen said, "But you could come to Spandles sometime in your car? Come and see me, I mean?"

"It's not my car, it's Jack's. But I can still walk. Do you mean that? About my coming to see you, I mean?"

"Of course. Why not?"

Joan shrugged. She still did not take her eyes off the straight, empty road. Helen wondered whether she was terrified of piling up Jack's car, and then thought that perhaps she just preferred talking that way. "Jack would have his reasons," she said. "But I'll come one of these days, you'll see. If you really mean it."

"Of course I mean it. Or should I come and pick you up?"

Joan said, "Ooh no," as if there were something outrageous in the suggestion. "But I like walking," she said. "Do you like walking?"

"Yes," said Helen, "but I haven't walked here much." This was not strictly true, because she had walked that very morning, only no one would ever know what had happened when she had.

For the first time Joan turned and looked at her. It was only a quick look, but unexpectedly penetrating. She said, "You will, you'll find," and once more Helen could not ask her what she meant by it.

When they came to where the Spandles drive turned off the road, Joan said, "I'll drop you here, if you don't mind. You can manage your basket to the house?"

Helen said, "Of course," but Joan had already stopped the car and backed it into the drive and turned out again onto the road facing towards the village. Helen got out and Joan handed her out her basket. Helen wanted to say something to re-establish contact, but Joan gave her no time. She waved a hand and set the car moving, and Helen said, "Good-bye and thank you," but did not think Joan would even have heard her.

She went along the drive slowly, with her heavy basket, thinking. Joan had said she would walk, and she had walked, and she had met Matthew Summers. No, that was not the order of it, quite. Joan had asked her if she walked, and she had said not, and that was untrue, because she had walked, and had met Matthew Summers. And then Joan had looked at her a little sharply, almost as if she smelt the prevarication, and had said she would walk, she'd see. But it would be only in her own mind that walking here was connected with Matthew Summers. There was no reason why it should be in Joan's. And she wished she had not prevaricated with Joan, and perhaps been disbelieved. She did not know why she had, except that she had already, at least by silence, prevaricated with Steve on the subject, and that seemed to commit her. But she did not see, in any way she was prepared to admit, why Matthew Summers should be able to impose this silence on people.

She was at the gate of the yard when her mind made the jump to the other thing that had been nagging at her since the day before. It was Matthew Summers who made the connection, and there was silence here too, in a way. She had it now. Celia had described him, talking to Steve mostly, as one of their leading Republicans, and then yesterday Charles had asked her what Celia had said about him, and she had been a bit puzzled, but had quoted the phrase when she had answered him. From something he said, Charles had clearly not heard it before, but had seemed to appreciate it, and then later, when Celia had come back, he had used it to her, and she had looked at him, with a quite expressionless face, for what had seemed quite a long time, and she herself had found it all a little disturbing, though at the time she had not been able to think why.

She still did not quite know why, except that now that she came to think of it, she felt sure that Charles had thrown the phrase at Celia deliberately, and although it had been her phrase to start with, she had not acknowledged it at all. She had not reacted in any way, only looked at Charles in silence with that deadpan face, and that had seemed odd, only now it seemed just another example of the way Matthew Summers imposed silence on people.

She opened the gate and shut it behind her, and went on across the yard. She tried to imagine herself saying to Steve, "Oh by the way, I met Mr. Summers this morning, and he said—" but after all what had he said that was worth repeating? She knew she would not in fact say anything of the sort to Steve. She could not imagine herself saying it at all.

Chapter 8

The river was not mentioned until late in the evening, and up to then the evening had been a good one. To Helen's mind unexpectedly good, because she had come to it with some apprehension, but from the moment they got there, everybody had been on their best behaviour. It was the men who mattered, of course. Apart from anything else, Steve and Charles were the only two of the four who had not met each other, and she had not looked forward to the meeting. She found herself increasingly worried about Steve's getting on with people at Ladon, and men had never been his strong suit. But he had made a dead set at both the Fearons from the start, and she had to admit he had managed it very well.

Her sense of relief, and her mere social enjoyment of the evening as such, did not prevent her thinking, in her moments of detachment, how interesting that was. That it was a calculated and disciplined effort on his part she had no doubt at all. He had not mentioned the party beforehand, and this was unusual in itself. He was generally full of explicit anticipation of parties, cheerful or otherwise. From her now established habit of mind, she felt convinced that he must have sensed her apprehension, and that made her feel guilty about it, as if she had somehow laid an unnecessary burden on him by her own misgivings. But it was not, in fact, unnecessary at all. Ladon was there and had to be coped with, and for them at least the Fearons seemed to be key figures in it, if, indeed, there was anyone in Ladon who was not. That was the difference between it and London, and it was a difference she had been afraid Steve would not understand. If he was going to work as hard at the rest of the village as he was working at the Fearons, perhaps she had been worrying too soon.

She could not remember, afterwards, quite how it had come up. Steve had been talking about his work, but only because Charles had asked him about it, and then with a mixture of proper diffidence and no-nonsense professionalism that she knew was carefully calculated, but could hardly have been bettered. He had said, with perfect truth, that he was working against time and was extremely busy, and had had no time to do anything much else. It would have been this that led to fishing, as one of the things he had not had time for. "All the same," he said, "I'm determined to have a go before the season's over. Lod must have fish in it." As he always did, he spoke of the river by its name, without the definite article, so that she almost expected him to call it "him," as he called his car "her." "But there doesn't seem to be much fishing done," he said. "You'd expect there to be in a place like this."

Charles said, "No, I don't think there is much."

Steve gave a small, sudden chuckle. "Perhaps they're afraid of Lod," he said. He looked at Charles, and Charles looked at him, and there was a moment of total silence.

Then Charles said, "Why should they be that?" He said it quietly in a completely non-committal voice, but he did not take his eyes off Steve.

Steve laughed again. "I wonder," he said. He thought for a moment. "I wonder," he said again. He was intent now, genuinely involved and no longer laughing. "I wonder if Lod's got a reputation as a river that has to take its lives? Some rivers have, you know. It goes back a very long way, but it still survives, even in these godless days. I mean, all rivers were gods once. I've never met it myself, or not up to now. Do they say that about Lod, would you know?"

Celia said, "Perhaps some rivers are just more dangerous than others."

Steve swung round in his chair to face her. She had spoken seriously, not making fun of him, but as it were calling him to order, and for a moment he looked at her equally seriously. Then his face relaxed into its warmest smile, so that she could not help smiling back at him, though Helen could have sworn that she did not really find much to smile at. "Oh good Lord," he said, "of course they are. Don't worry. You won't find me chucking a chicken in to make the river stay away from my door. I don't believe a river needs propitiating. I think it needs watching and its banks kept in order. I don't believe that if the witches stop dancing their round dances, the sun will stop going round the sky. But I believe there are still people who do believe it. At any rate, I hope there are. I like things to go on. Don't you?"

It was Celia who was unsmiling now. She looked at him very straight. "Only some things," she said.

Charles said, "I think you may find that the reason why people don't fish here is that they can't. I mean, not without poaching. If you come to think of it, the whole river frontage in Ladon parish is in Mr. Summers' hands. The eastern half is Spandles land and the western's Calton, and he holds them both. I can't see people poaching on Matthew Summers."

"Good Lord," said Steve. It was a favourite exclamation of his. His boyishness had a slightly period flavour, perhaps because boyishness itself was out of fashion, even among boys. "Good Lord, I hadn't thought of that. I knew he had the Spandles grazing, of course. I didn't think about the fishing."

Charles smiled at him. It was a curiously gentle smile, so that Helen wondered for a moment whether he was actually going to like him. "Well, you look it up," he said. "I think you'll find I'm right."

Steve said, "But old Wetherby fished. He was fishing when he fell in, or so I gathered."

"Wetherby had the land. He had a right to fish."

"And then he was drowned, and Matthew Summers took over the land and the fishing?"

"I imagine so, yes."

"But he doesn't fish himself?"

"Not that I know of."

"Well, perhaps he'll let me fish if I ask him nicely? I shan't poach, anyhow."

Charles still spoke with that curiously light touch, as if he was somehow speaking to the boy Steve was somehow pretending to be. "No," he said, "I shouldn't poach. But you could ask him, certainly."

Steve nodded. "I will," he said. He thought for a moment. "So if I were to buy Spandles, I'd have to buy the land with it to get the fishing?"

There was another moment's silence. Then Charles said, "Were you thinking of buying Spandles?" and Steve looked at Helen with the slightest touch of defiance. Then he looked first at Celia and then at Charles with a sort of mischievous smile that did not quite work. "I'm toying with the idea, certainly," he said. "I got the impression the owners would be glad enough to sell."

"I don't know who the owners are," said Charles. "I know it was sold after Wetherby's death, but the house has stood empty ever since, and of course Summers took over the land."

"Some sort of a company," said Steve. "I got the impression that they'd bought Spandles as a speculation and found it a bit of a white elephant."

This time it was Charles who nodded. "That may be," he said. "They might sell the house at that, if you really thought of buying. Whether they'd sell the land I don't know. I fancy if it came to that, you'd find Summers in against you."

Steve smiled again, shrugging it off. "Oh well," he said, "we're in the house for the moment, and very nice too. And I'll ask Summers about the fishing."

"All right," said Charles, "but don't push it if he doesn't seem too keen. It's for him to say, after all."

Steve did not like this. Helen was not sure whether he did not like the suggestion that Mr. Summers might refuse, or whether it was the mere fact that Charles had presumed to advise him, and about Mr. Summers, of all people. She could not tell whether the others noticed it, but to her that sudden slight lift of the head was unmistakable, and when he spoke, the pitch of his voice was just a shade higher. "Oh quite," he said, "quite."

For a moment Charles went on looking at him, and then his face relaxed, and he turned and smiled at Helen, and the chill went out of the air, and the party re-gathered itself to finish as it had begun. "Well," Charles said, "what about a nightcap before you go? You haven't far to drive."

She wondered whether Steve would return to the subject of the fishing and Mr. Summers later, when they got home, or even on the way home. If he did not, it would mean that he felt strongly about it, and was already, consciously or unconsciously, calculating his chances and wondering whether to risk a rebuff. A rebuff from Mr. Summers would be worse than no fishing. If he decided not to risk it, he would find good neighbourly reasons for not asking, or more likely build up the act of working against time so that the question of fishing simply did not arise. She knew nothing about fishing seasons, but he had implied that the season, whatever it was, was running out, and he would not have to keep it up for long.

He did not mention it. When they were out of the side-street and onto the road, he said, "What nice people," keeping up the warmth of the party, and she knew that when they got home, they would go to bed at once, and he would make love to her. He always made love to her after a successful party. She also knew that he felt strongly about the fishing, and wondered, with a curious touch of anxiety, what he would decide to do about it.

When she got up the next morning, the mist was on the fields again, but Steve would be awake and up soon, because he had not worked late the night before, and, fishing or no fishing, he was genuinely pressed for time. She knew he would sooner issue a dud cheque than default on a deadline, even if, as might well be the case, it was a deadline he had set himself. She recognised, as she always had, the admirable qualities in him. It was just that she was beginning to doubt whether they were in themselves enough. She put on her dressing-gown and went downstairs to make the tea. She did not notice the ticking of the clock, because Steve might already be awake upstairs and waiting for his tea, or if he was not, he soon would be. She did not feel even constructively alone in the house, and the clock had nothing to say to her. It was only when she was starting to put the teathings on the tray that she put down a cup suddenly on the table, where it was, under her hand, and stood for a moment stock still while she considered the implications of the way her mind had been working. It had gone straight from the sight of the mist to the fact that today Steve would not be sleeping late, and the association had been a negative one, the second term somehow contradicting the first. The unmistakable suggestion was that if Steve had been sleeping late, or had somehow not been there, she would have gone out walking in the mist as she had before. She would have walked, as Joan Winthrop had told her she would, and she would have walked on Matthew Summers' land, because all the land between the road and the river was his, and he had told her that if she came onto his ground, she must expect to meet him. Why she should meet him, in all those acres of grass, when you could not see more than a few yards in any direction, she did not know, but she assumed she would, just as she assumed that he was already out there now, some-

where under the mist, walking on his ground. Perhaps his
dark eyes could see in the mist in a way hers could not, or
perhaps he could hear her moving when she could not hear
him. Only today she was not going out, because Steve was
awake upstairs and waiting for his tea, and that was a thing
Mr. Summers would seem to know about. She put the things
together hastily on the tray, tightened the girdle of her
dressing-gown, which had worked loose as she stood there
leaning on the table, and opened the kitchen door and took
the tray quickly up the silent stairs, breathing a little faster
than the easy pitch of the stairs gave her real reason to.

They got up and breakfasted quickly, because Steve was
in a hurry to get to work, as she had known he would be,
but by the time they had finished, and he had gone upstairs
to his south-eastern room, the mist was already off the fields.
She left the washing-up for the moment and went up to their
bedroom, which was on the other side of the house, with its
door facing Steve's. Steve's door was shut, and she shut the
bedroom door after her, and went over to the window and
stood there looking out, with the two shut doors between
them. There had been no sun today to clear the mist, only a
small damp breeze from the south, which had blown the
mist off the fields and brought a thin grey cast of cloud over
the whole sky. The light was wan and rather cheerless, but
she could see everything very clearly, what there was to see.
She saw that there were cattle grazing on two of the fields
between her and the river. Whether they were the fields
next to the bank she could not be sure, because she could
not see the river itself, but from the distance and the fences
she thought they must be. If they were a milking herd, it
meant that twice a day someone would have to come from
Calton and call them in and count heads and open gates for
them, but she could not see from here if they were. At this
time of the year the heifers and stores looked grown beasts
at this distance. There was no one with them now.

She turned her back on the window and then, at a

thought, went over and opened the door before she got on with making the bed and tidying the room. Steve's door was still shut, and no sound came from behind it. He did not work direct onto a typewriter, but wrote with a ball-point in his own small handwriting, which looked orderly because the lines were straight and evenly spaced, but was rather ill-formed and untidy in detail. When she had finished the room, she went downstairs to do the washing-up and think about her shopping. She would not see Steve now until he came downstairs for coffee at eleven, and not then if she was out when he came down. She liked the house much more than she had the flat, because there was much more space and she could never think that living all on one floor was altogether natural, but it meant a lot more work, and she must think about getting someone to help her with the cleaning. She thought she could ask Celia about that, and then she thought that she would do far better to ask Joan Winthrop, who would be more likely to know of someone. She might go and see her when she had done her shopping. She had not walked today, and could meet Joan's eye if she had to.

She did not drive into the garage yard at all, but stopped the car on the roadside in front of the Winthrops' bungalow. She did not have to have Jack's permission to go and visit his wife. The front door opened almost before she was out of her car, and Joan was on the step looking at her. For a moment she almost let herself believe that her visit was expected. All villages knew what you had done, or even what you were doing. Ladon seemed to have a fair idea of what you were going to do. Then she had the less extravagant picture of Joan, alone and bored in her four-room bungalow, longing for a contact with the outside world and running to the window at the first sound of a car stopping. Perhaps she had not anticipated her visit, only hoped for it. At any rate, there she was, smiling at her as she came up the concrete strip from the neatly painted gate to the neatly painted door. She said, "Oh Mrs. Anderson, I'm so glad you've come. Do come in."

As she might have expected, knowing the Winthrops, the furniture and decoration were much better than the bungalow itself, as easy to her eye as the Fearons' and much better looked after. Joan had a working husband out all day, not an invalid always at home, or even, as she herself had, a working husband at home most of the time. No wonder she was bored. She got coffee, also better than seemed likely, and when Helen broached the subject of her visit, her reaction was totally unexpected. She sat straight up in her chair, staring at Helen with wide eyes. Then the eyes flicked sideways in the direction of the garage and came back to Helen's again. "Oh," she said, "I wonder if Jack would let me come?"

Helen said, "You yourself?" She was genuinely surprised, but she also felt an instinct to exaggerate her surprise, as if to make it clear that this was not what she had had in mind.

"Well, why not? I haven't got half enough to do here, and I'm good about the house."

"My dear, I can see that. But I mean—would you like to? I hadn't thought—"

"Oh I'd love it, if he'd let me."

"Well, do ask him. It wouldn't be every day, of course. Say two or three mornings a week, at whatever the going rate is. And I could come and fetch you and run you back. You wouldn't need your car." She meant Jack's car, but did not say so.

"That would be lovely," Joan said. "And I could do with the money, to tell the truth." She said "I," not "we," and in Helen's mind another small bit of the picture slipped into place.

"Well look," she said, "you talk to Jack and let me know." She wondered whether she ought to have said "your husband," when she had not even called Joan "Joan" yet, but it did not seem to matter. "I do hope you can manage it. Spandles is more than I really want to manage by myself, and it would be nice to have you."

Joan put her cup down with a clink and got up. "I'm coming," she said. "When do I start? I don't really think Jack'll mind, but if he does, he'll just have to get over it."

Helen got up too. "Well, if you're sure," she said, "let's say Monday. I'll fetch you at—what?—half past nine, or would that be too early? But only if you're sure. I don't want to upset Jack."

"Oh it wouldn't be you he'd be upset with. That wouldn't be Jack at all. And half past nine would be fine."

"All right, then. Half past nine on Monday. But let me know if you change your mind."

Joan laughed and shook her head, and Helen suddenly saw her as one of those soft women with a sort of elastic strength, quite different from herself. "No one's going to change my mind," she said, and Helen took herself off.

She had not spoken to Steve about it before she left. He had been busy, and she had not expected to get anything settled so soon. But there would be no trouble there. He was never mean over money, and liked to have the house looking nice. He would like having Joan about the place, too. For the matter of that, almost any man would, but with Steve in particular to have the only other pretty woman in the village as his daily would add to his picture of himself. She left her car in the yard and went upstairs to tell him.

It took her some minutes to convince herself that he was not in the house. He so seldom went out during the morning. She had not noticed whether his car was in the garage, and was going to the back door to see when she heard it come into the yard. She opened the door and met him as he came in. He was looking extraordinarily cheerful, almost in a way triumphant. She said, "Oh there you are. Look, I hope you don't mind. I've fixed with Mrs. Winthrop to come in a few mornings a week and give me a hand with the house.

We really need someone, with a place of this size. Will that be all right?"

He said, "What? Oh yes, rather, that'll be fine." He seemed hardly to give the matter a thought, as if he had something else on his mind that he was waiting to tell her.

They went into the kitchen, and Helen started to unpack her shopping, which she had dumped on the table before she hurried upstairs to give him the news. For a moment he stood watching her. Then he said, "I've been over to Calton to ask Summers about the fishing."

Helen froze where she was and looked at him. She felt suddenly hollow, as if the wind had been knocked out of her. But he was waiting for her to ask him, and with an effort she found her voice. "Oh yes?" she said. "What did he say?"

Steve said, "Oh it's perfectly all right. No trouble at all. He seemed pleased rather than otherwise. He's a funny chap."

She said, "Oh good," and he went out of the kitchen and upstairs to his room. He smiled as he went. For quite a while she stood there, still motionless, wondering what it was that was upsetting her so.

Chapter 9

For once in a way, Steve woke before she did, and when she did wake, she heard him whistling in the bathroom. He had got up and gone along the passage without waking her, but he had left the bedroom door open. It was an extremely cheerful whistle, all bits and pieces, so that it was impossible to make any tune out of it. He had been cheerful all the evening before, and he was still cheerful. It was getting his own way over the fishing, of course, not so much the fishing itself as getting what he wanted out of Mr. Summers. Especially, unless she was mistaken, after Charles' warning. He liked to see himself as a man who admitted of no obstacles, but she knew he measured obstacles very carefully before he let them come in his path. She fancied that yesterday morning, while she had been out shopping and talking to Joan Winthrop, he had been engaged, behind his shut door, in a fairly agonised debate, and she imagined him, having made his decision, rushing off straight away to put it to the touch, so that he could put the thing out of his head and get on with his work. It was even possible that he had deliberately taken advantage of her absence to save explanations, and she wondered whether, if Mr. Summers had refused him, he would even have told her where he had been. He was curiously devious about things that were too small to give her any real cause for complaint.

She wondered about Mr. Summers, too, but then she found herself spending a good deal of time wondering about him. She wondered now whether he had really seemed pleased, as Steve had said he had, and if so, why. In particular, she wondered whether it was anything to do with her, and then told herself that this was nonsense, but still did not quite believe it was. She was up and in her dressing-gown by the time Steve came back from the bathroom. He was still whistling. She said, "Hullo. Sorry I overslept a bit. Shall I get some tea?"

"Not for me, thanks. I had a quick cup when I got up. You go and get yourself some. There's no hurry about breakfast."

She smiled, partly in simple response to his cheerfulness, but also because it was all so perfectly in character. He would not mind in the least getting himself tea while she slept on, but it would never occur to him to get tea for her while he was getting it for himself. He fitted his own world comfortably round hers, but did not go out of his way to include her in it. She said, "All right. I won't be long," and went downstairs, leaving him to his dressing.

When she came upstairs, he was in his room, but the door was open, and presently he came across to her, dressed for the day, and reciting to himself in a fair imitation of the local speech. He said,

> "Lod will take, or cost you dear,
> A life at every second year."

She stopped what she was doing and stared at him, suddenly appalled. She said, "Where in God's name did you hear that?"

He laughed at her consternation, still indefeasibly cheerful. "I didn't," he said. "I made it up. But it's right in the tradition." He went into broad West-Country.

> "River Dart, River Dart,
> Every year thou claim'st a heart.

"That I didn't make up. Dart's a greedy river. But then it's got a tidal estuary and plenty of silly summer visitors.

Trent's even greedier. Trent takes three a year. But then Trent has the eagre, which is the name of a once-respected Norse god. The locals still call the eagre 'him,' or did till recently. Dee's as bad." This time he went into music-hall Scots.

"Bloodthirsty Dee each year takes three,
But bonnie Don, he takes none.

"I don't know what makes Don so undemanding. Perhaps somebody caught him unawares and christened him. But I still think the locals are afraid of Lod. It's all very well for Charles to say they're afraid of Summers, but they could have asked him. I found him easy enough." He smiled into her still wide open eyes. "Oh go on with you," he said. "Lod's given you the creeps a bit from the start. There's nothing to look like that about. I told you, I only made up the one about Lod." He came over to her and kissed her lightly. "Give me a shout when breakfast's ready," he said. He turned and went back into his room, and this time the door shut behind him.

He talked about fishing over breakfast, and by the time he had gone upstairs to his work, she knew it would not be long before he got out his gear and made a start at it. It was still not so much the fishing itself that appealed to him as the fact that he was allowed to fish. He would want that established. She would not put it past him even to allow himself to appear in the village in full fishing rig, just in case nobody actually saw him on the bank, and the word did not get round. Equally, on the other side, once he had established his right to fish, he might not in fact do very much fishing, especially if the fishing turned out to be poor, and he did not catch much. Then his genuine and sensible preoccupation with his work would soon oust his slightly suspect passion for fishing, and he would not have much more time to give to it.

She did not really want him fishing at all. She could not

get it out of her head that there was danger in it. Of all things, she could not get out of her head the noise her stone had made dropping into that silent, unseen water, and she remembered the straight lip of turf, cut off clean as if with a knife, and for all she knew undercut by the gnawing of the water under it. She did not believe, any more than he did, that it was all Mr. Summers' doing that the village people did not fish there. Even Charles had said it was dangerous, and he had never seen it. He could have got that only from hearsay. She suspected that Charles, like other people in his position, took an intense interest in the affairs of his neighbours. She thought he probably engaged in long talks with the postman and other people who came to the house, who would indulge him because they were sorry for him, and because they were ensnared, as she had been, by his tremendous charm. She wanted to have another talk to Charles, if only to reassure herself. She went about her business in the house in a slightly perfunctory way, secure already in the knowledge that by Monday she would have Joan there to fill the gaps she left. Then she got her shopping bag, and put on a coat because it was no longer warm, and went to get her car out. She had shopping to do, but she knew where she was going when she had done it.

It was still the same cheerless weather. There was no mist on the fields now, and no sun to clear it if there had been. Everything looked dark and clear-cut in the dead white light, and the chill southerly breeze moved steadily between the dark earth and the wan sky. It was not the weather for this landscape. The post van came down the drive as she went into the yard, a spot of moving colour in a dead world, and it might be a messenger from other worlds that still had the sun on them. She took a couple of letters for herself and dropped them into her shopping bag. They did not look important. Steve's mail, which was always numerous and tended to look important, she took inside and put on the kitchen table. That was standard practice when he was working. Coming at this hour, the post might always break up his valued first spell of the day, and he refused to look at it until he came downstairs for his coffee. Then she went out into the yard again and on an impulse, before she went to her car, went through the small gate and along the west wall of the house to the top of the front garden.

She stood there, staring south across the fields towards the river, looking for something, she did not know what. She saw nothing but the fields. Even the cattle had gone. If there had been a figure moving on the bank, she could have seen it, but there was none. It occurred to her that if Steve fished from the Spandles land, she could see him, in clear weather, most of the way, and she had a momentary picture of herself watching him, perhaps even with a pair of field-glasses from a top window. She rejected the picture at once as preposterous. Not that, at all costs. That way madness lay. Then, just before she turned, she wondered whether she would one day, from here, see the river itself, and what it would look like when she saw it. She imagined a gleam of reflected light where before there had been nothing but the fields, because the river would have climbed out of its tunnel and be starting to move her way. She would see it, of course, one of these days, if it happened in daylight, because the river apparently flooded the fields to some extent at some point every year. She did not like the thought of it any better.

She turned and went back to the gate, and as she went Steve's damnable little rhyme came into her head.

> Lod will take, or cost you dear,
> A life at every seventh year.

She shut the gate behind her and went and got into the car. Then, as she settled herself in the driving seat, she thought, but that was not right. That was not Steve's rhyme exactly. He had said "second." It was she who had made it "seventh." She knew why, too. She had been thinking, subconsciously, of old Wetherby. She backed the car out with un-accustomed violence and drove fast for the village.

Even Charles was not sitting outside today. He was in the sitting-room, and Celia was with him. They seemed pleased to see her, and Celia went across to the kitchen to make the coffee. The doors were opposite and both open. Charles said, "Where's Steve? What's he up to? Too busy to come?"

She looked at her watch. She said, "Well, at this particular moment he'll be in the kitchen, making himself coffee and opening his post. But that's just a break. He's been working since about nine, in fact, and he'll be back on the job again when I get back. He won't take long off, unless there's something in the post that stops him, but that would probably be work of a sort too. He does work for his money, you know."

"Good for him. And does he keep that up all day?"

"Well," she said, "he does generally. I mean, when he's rushed like this. This afternoon I rather suspect he's going fishing."

Charles' head went up with a jerk. "Is he?" he said. "I really don't think that's wise. Summers won't like it."

She said with elaborate casualness, "Oh that's all right. Steve's asked him. He didn't mind at all."

She was suddenly aware that Celia had come across from the kitchen and was standing in the doorway, listening. For what seemed quite a long time neither she nor Charles said anything. Then Charles said, "Well I'm damned." He said it very quietly, as if he had been alone in the room and something outside in the street had surprised him. He was not even looking at her now.

From the doorway Celia said, "When was this, then?"

Helen kept determinedly to her casual tone. She did not feel casual in the least. She would have watched the pair of them if she could, but they were one on each side of her. She answered Celia's question, but kept her eyes on Charles.

She said, "Oh yesterday. Yesterday morning. He went and saw him at Calton."

Celia said, "*He* went? You weren't with him?"

She shook her head. She was still watching Charles. "No, no," she said, "I was in the village, shopping and seeing Joan Winthrop."

She wondered whether her mention of Joan would distract their attention, but it did not. Charles lifted his eyes from his hands and looked at her. "How did he take it? Summers, I mean. Did Steve tell you?"

"Oh yes. He said there was no trouble at all. He said Mr. Summers seemed quite pleased."

Charles moved his head in what was almost a shrug. "Well," he said, "that's all right, then," but she did not believe he really thought it was all right. Celia went back into the kitchen without saying anything, and she could hear her putting the coffee things on the tray. She had got what she wanted, which was their immediate, unprompted reaction. She did not like it much, but she had got it. Now she could come out with what was really in her mind, and for the moment she had Charles to herself.

She said, "Charles, is it really dangerous? The river, I mean. You said it was."

He looked at her very straight and spoke very carefully. "Well, look, my dear," he said, "I only know what I'm told. I've never even seen the damned thing. But people do say it is, yes."

She said, "What, the flooding and all that?" She knew it was not the flooding he was thinking of. She wanted to know about the flooding, but she could get back to that later. For the moment she did not want to lead him.

"Oh well, no," he said. "The floods don't come all that quick. We don't have a tidal bore or anything. We're too far upstream for that."

"A bore?" she said. "Is that the same as an eagre?"

He looked at her, wrinkling his brow. "An eagre?" he said.

"Yes, I think it is, more or less, but the eagre's on some particular river or rivers, I forget which."

"Trent, for one. I know, I've heard Steve mention it."

He nodded. "Well, anyhow, it's not that. No, I think it's more the banks. And the river itself, of course. They say the banks aren't safe, and if the bank lets you down, the river itself is nasty. Especially if it's in spate. Mind you, if someone was merely walking down by the river, calling the cattle home or something, he wouldn't want to walk right on the edge of the bank anyhow. There's no reason why he should. But a fisherman's different, especially when he's got something on his line, and is excited. He'd want to see all the water, and ten to one he wouldn't look where he was putting his feet. I assume that's what happened with old Wetherby, and I don't think there's been much fishing done since. Steve's a different proposition, obviously. He's young and strong, and I'd think in fact, despite all his get-up-and-go, he's naturally cautious. But he ought to be warned, all the same. Tell him so from me, if you think that would do any good."

She knew it would not do any good. She knew it was as much as anything Charles' last warning that had sent Steve, for all his natural caution, which Charles had unexpectedly but quite correctly recognised, rushing to Calton, risking a rebuff that would have upset him very badly indeed. And if the warning came from her, he would only say it was Lod giving her the creeps again. But it was no good telling Charles all that. She nodded and said, "I'll tell him," and then Celia brought in the coffee.

As she poured it out, she said, "Did you say you'd seen Joan Winthrop?" So it had not gone unnoticed after all.

"Yes, that's right. I'd met her before, of course, when I took my car there. She's going to come and give me a hand in the house."

Charles said, "What, pretty Joan? Is she, by Jove? Steve's

pretty favoured in his attendant angels, I must say. Will she be any good to you, though?"

Charles was doing the talking, but Helen knew that it was Celia, the silent Celia, who was watching her now. She said, "Oh I think so, certainly. Her own house is spotless. And I think she's bored. To tell the truth, it never occurred to me to ask her to come herself. I really went to ask her if she knew of anyone, but she suggested coming herself, and, I must say, I jumped at it. She's starting on Monday." She turned to Celia. "You must tell me what I ought to pay her, by the way. I don't know what the going rates are round here."

Celia said, "Nor do I," and there was a moment's silence. Then she smiled. "But I'll find out, of course. You can't very well ask about it yourself, when people will know who it is you're going to be paying." She drank some of her coffee. Then she said, "What does Jack think of it?"

Helen was all innocence. She was not giving away any of Joan's secrets. "I don't know," she said. "I don't imagine he'd mind. It won't be all that much, after all. Two or three mornings a week, I think. And they've only got a tiny house and no family. I don't think Jack will suffer."

Celia nodded but said nothing, and Helen turned to Charles again. "Tell me about the floods," she said. "Do they come every year? And what's involved?"

"Most years, I think. They miss sometimes. But it's not generally anything very dramatic. Just the fields along the river, and not very deep there. I mean, it's not Sands of Dee stuff. You know— 'The feet had scarcely time to flee, When all the world was in the sea.'" Helen thought, bloodthirsty Dee. But that was a different Dee, of course. Charles' was *High Tide on the Lincolnshire Coast*. She remembered it now. "I mean," said Charles, "if Steve was fishing, he wouldn't suddenly find himself up to his waist in water. He'd have plenty of time to pack up his gear and be off home. And anyhow, people generally know it's coming. You only have to keep an eye eastwards. If there's heavy rain on the hills there, you know the water's got to come this way. But so far as this parish is concerned, it's really only Summers who's at any risk, especially now he's got the Spandles land as well. It's all grazing, I mean, along the river, and I suppose he's got to get his beasts off it in time."

Helen said, "He's got them off it now. At least, off the Spandles land. I noticed this morning."

"Has he? Well, it may not mean anything. But he may have an idea it's coming. He'd know if anyone would, and we're getting to the right time of the year, in fact." He thought for a moment. "Of course," he said, "he's the one at risk in another way too. I mean if there was a really serious flood. Calton's quite a bit lower than the village. I mean, the actual buildings. They're a bit higher than the land round them, and even a moderate flood can cut them off for a bit. But if the water ever came up to the village again, he'd have several feet of water in his ground-floor rooms, I imagine. And of course in his yards and buildings too, and if he'd got all his stock in, as I suppose he would have, it wouldn't be funny."

"But has it ever happened, do you know?"

"Well, in the past it must have. The famous 1839 one must have pretty well cleared out Calton, I should think. And I think there was a fairly bad one just before our time. Eight or nine years ago, that would be. But nothing since." He looked across at Helen, sensing the anxiety in her. "But you don't have to worry about Spandles," he said. "You sit well up. The whole village would have to be under water before it reached you—the house, I mean. And you haven't got any stock to worry about."

Helen said, "Well, thank goodness for that." She turned and found Celia watching her, always with the same wide-eyed, dead-pan face. She thought Celia knew more than Charles. Celia knew too much altogether, and she wondered how and why. She got up and gathered her things together.

"I must be going," she said. "Steve will be wanting his lunch, whatever he decides to do this afternoon."

Celia came out with her to see her off. When they were outside, she said, "You're lucky to get Joan, I think. I know Charles talks of her as if she were just a little bit of fluff, but she's not that, not by a long chalk."

"No," said Helen. "No. I don't think she is." They looked at each other for a moment, and then Helen got into her car and took herself off.

When she got in, Steve was already downstairs. She said, "Hullo, sorry I'm a bit late. I dropped in on Charles and Celia." She was not in fact late at all, it was Steve who was early, but she always found it easier to apologise.

"That's all right," he said. "There's no hurry. Look, I've heard from Peter." Peter was his agent, and the way he spoke suggested something of importance.

"Oh yes?" she said. "Good news, I hope?"

"I think so, yes, but I've got to go and have a talk with him. I thought I'd go up tomorrow, and get a bed at the club or somewhere. Then I could see him on Monday morning and be back here in the evening. Will that be all right?"

She said, "Yes, of course." She had wondered when this was going to happen, and could not see why she should feel so breathless about it now it had. "You won't have to go off early tomorrow?"

"Good Lord, no. I'll go up after lunch and take my time." He looked at her and smiled. He was suddenly jubilant again. "And after lunch today," he said, "I'm going fishing."

Chapter 10

It was only when she went out to see Steve off that she realised how dark the day had got. They often had lights on in the kitchen in grey weather, because it faced north and east, and the out-buildings and the walls of the kitchen garden stood close up to the windows. Once the lights were on, the room was lit like an operating theatre, and it was difficult to judge what was going on outside. They had been on today since soon after breakfast, and between getting clear of a late breakfast and getting ready an early lunch she had not been out of the kitchen much. Now, with lunch over and Steve ready to go, she had expected to find the passage dark, but was shaken to find how dark it still was even when they opened the back door and went out into the yard. The breeze had died down and it felt less cold, but overhead the sky, leaden and motionless, was there almost for the touching.

Steve looked up at it for a moment, shrugged, and put his suitcase in the back of the car and his briefcase and coat on the passenger seat in front. "Going to be a wet drive before I've gone very far," he said. "It's coming up from the south-east by the look of it. Look at that." He nodded over her shoulder, and when she turned, she saw that the whole sky on that side was almost slate-blue, like a sky full of snow, only it was not nearly cold enough for snow yet. She remembered what Charles had said about watching the hills to eastwards, but she did not think that, even from upstairs, there would be any hills to be seen.

"Well, be careful," she said, and Steve laughed. He was still in the highest good humour. He had come back at tea-time the day before with two small fish—first-fruits, he called them—which had gone into the freezer to await his return. He had found that the river opened out into what was almost a pool farther west, whether on Calton land or Spandles he was not sure. He had got there too late to do much good with it, but he had high hopes of it, and was going straight to it when next he went out. It had kept him cheerful all the evening, and now he was cheerful, though he did not say so, because he was going to London. Whether he had high hopes of that too, or whether he was merely glad to be getting away to it she was not sure. It could be both.

"Oh I'll be careful," he said. "I always am. You know that," and she had to admit it was true. "Look after yourself," he said.

She smiled equally cheerfully, partly because it was the correct response, and partly because she knew she did not at all mind having the place to herself for a bit. "I will," she said. "And anyhow, I'll have Joan to look after me tomorrow morning."

His eyebrows went up. "So you will," he said. "I'd forgotten. And I'll be back in the evening." They exchanged friendly kisses, and he got into the car and was off. She waved after the car once as it went off along the drive, and then turned and went back into the house.

It was preternaturally quiet, and when she went into the kitchen, she heard the ticking of the clock at once. This was nonsense, because most of the time when Steve was in the house he made no sound at all. But she knew it was nothing really to do with other sounds. She heard the clock when time was her own, as it never could be when Steve was in the house. She remembered Joan's saying, "Oh time, I've got plenty of time," and yet Jack was only at the other end of the yard, and there was a telephone line in between. It was something to do with detachment. Joan had detached herself consciously from Jack. She could say, "Oh that's Jack all over," speaking of him to a woman she had only just met in a way she sometimes caught herself thinking of Steve but would never express to anyone else. Or never had yet. Perhaps she would come to that, too. She wondered about Celia. Celia expressed so little. She asked and looked and kept her thoughts to herself, including her thoughts about Charles. Meanwhile Steve was away on the road to London, getting farther away every minute, and the clock ticked for her alone.

But the lunch things were all over the table, Steve's things as well as her own, and she set about clearing them and washing them up and putting them away. When she had done that, the kitchen would be her own, as time was, until tomorrow evening. No, not until tomorrow evening, because tomorrow morning Joan would be there. She was not sure she welcomed that, with Steve away, but she would have to see. Meanwhile she got the lunch things out of the way, and then went up to the bedroom and looked out of the window. She looked out across the fields towards the river, because there was nothing else to look at. Except that out of the west window, even in this light, she could just see, away across the fields, the roofs of Calton. She stood there for quite a time looking at them. Then she turned and went out of the room. The room was not hers, anyway. It was Steve's as well. Steve had his own room across the landing, but she had no room of her own. She went across and opened the door and looked in. She looked at Steve's room for quite a time, but she did not want to go into it when he was away. It was superficially orderly but untidy in detail, like his writing. She shut the door and went downstairs to the sitting-room, and sat in the comfortable chair that was, by prescription, hers, more wholly hers than the bedroom was upstairs. She sat there, relaxed, and let her own time flow over her.

She woke with a start. She must have slept quite deeply, because she had been dreaming of something that had completely absorbed her. She could not remember what it was, but it had been wholly hers. She looked at her watch and found it was tea-time, but she did not want tea. She felt restless now she was awake, because she could not even remember her dream, let alone get back into it. She went out into the passage behind the kitchen and put on her mackintosh and gumboots, and tied a headscarf over her hair. Then she opened the back door and went out into the yard.

It did not seem to be any darker now than it had when Steve left, and it still had not rained. If it started to rain, she could turn and come home. Dressed as she was, she ought not to get very wet, and if she did, it did not matter. She could dry her clothes and warm herself in her own time. She went round the west side of the house, along the garden and down the steps into the fields. The grass was dry underfoot and the going firm. She turned, not due south, but south-westwards, on a slant across the fenced fields, that would bring her to the river some way west of the house, if she kept going long enough. She could see where she was going now. There was no need for her to grope her way along the fences. She kept going steadily, crossed several fences on a slant, and then turned to look back at the house. It stood up clearly, looking almost black against the dark sky. It occurred to her that she ought to have left some lights on, in case the dusk shut down before she was home, but she was not going back now. She turned and went on again. Now that she could see all round her, the distances did not seem as big as they had in her imagination when she could not. Going as she was, on that firm, flat grassland, it was all well within her compass. She would walk as far as she wanted to, and then turn and go home. Time was her own. Only she would not cross the last fence above the river. She was not walking towards Calton, but she could see it, if she looked, away in front of her and to her right. It looked no farther from her now than Spandles was behind.

It was only when she was in the last field before the river that she turned to look back at Spandles and found she could no longer see it. She knew it was there, in her line of sight, but she could no longer see it, and when she turned to look at Calton, she could not see that either. It must have got dark very suddenly, either because the unseen sun had gone down or because the cloud cover overhead had thickened. She felt a moment of disquiet, but no sense of panic. What did occur to her was that it might be going to rain. At any rate, it was time she turned for home. She had only to keep crossing the fences at about the same angle, and she would see the house again. She stopped and half-turned, and then, away in front of her, not very far away, something let out a long, agonising cry of distress. It was all on one high, sustained note. It was not a human cry, but she could not think what kind of animal it could be. She stopped, suddenly appalled, and then it came again. She could not see what was making it, but it was not very far away. Whatever it was, she could not leave it and turn and go home with that cry following her. She hurried towards the sound and then, after a bit, started to run. When the cry came again, she realised that it was a cow. It could be nothing else, but she had never before heard a cow make a noise like that.

She came on it quite suddenly, because it was now too dark to see anything that was not quite close at hand. At the same moment she came to the fence above the river. She came to them together, because the cow was tied to one of the posts carrying the fence. It had stopped crying now, but was struggling to get free, wrenching its head ineffectively against the rope that was fastened round its neck. The other end was tied to the post. It was not choking or in any obvious physical trouble, and cows must be used to being tied up. She could not understand its desperation, but she was a little frightened by it. She spoke to it, trying to calm it, as she came up. She had never had much to do with cows at close quarters, but she spoke to it as she would have spoken to any other animal in distress, or for that matter any human. At any rate, it stopped struggling and stood there, panting a little, and staring at her in the gloom with its large, dark eyes. She went to the post and started wrestling with the knot in the rope.

It was tied very tight in what felt like a nylon rope, and she could not see it clearly enough to be certain how to work on it, even if her fingers were strong enough for the job. She cast round in her mind for some way of cutting the rope, but there was only grass and posts and wire, and she did not, as Steve would have done, carry a knife on her. She went back to the knot again, and then the cow lifted its head and let out that long terrible wail, as if the help at hand had failed it and it was calling again to other help from far off. The noise died away, and then it lowered its head and started to pull madly at the rope again, snatching it out of her fingers and making it impossible for her to work on the knot. She staggered and found her feet in their boots somehow obstructed, and when she looked down, she saw there was water up to her ankles. She turned and looked over her shoulder, and the dark cleft where the river should have been was no longer there. Instead there was a broad level surface, gleaming dully in the last light from the sky, and stretching from where she stood as far as she could see into the encroaching darkness.

Her blind instinct was to run, but she could not leave the cow where it was. She screamed at it, begging it to stand still, and something of her desperation must have got through to it. It stopped tugging at the rope and turned and looked at her, and as it turned, she felt wetness on first one foot and then the other, and knew the water was into her boots. For a few moments longer the terrified creature stood quiet, only a few moments, but just long enough for her to see her mistake. There was no need to untie the knot. The rope was tied in a loop, and the loop was dropped over the head of the post and rested on the top strand of wire. The cow could not get it off, because it could only pull downwards. If something lifted the beast bodily, as she supposed the river itself might, the rope might be lifted off the post, only then it would be too late. But she could lift it, if only the cow would let her. She dragged the loop upwards towards the top of the post, but was still a few inches short. She screamed at the cow again, pulling desperately on the taut rope, and then its head came round a little more, and the loop slipped off the post and on to her forearm, almost up to the elbow. A moment later the cow plunged forward again, and this time she went with it, splashing and struggling at its flank through the dark, encumbering water.

For a moment she was panic-stricken and struggled to get the rope off her arm, but saw just in time that this was the last thing she must do. The cow was her only hope now. She had saved it, and now only it could save her. It was stronger and heavier than she was, and it had four feet to her two, and above all it would know where to go, which she, in the now almost total darkness, could not. She bent her elbow and hugged her arm to her, concentrating desperately on keeping her feet under her. The cow went forward at a sort of lumbering gallop, and she ran with it, breathing in sobs and willing herself, above all, not to let it drag her off her feet. She could not have told, afterwards, how long this went on, but at last, just when she was at the end of her endurance, the cow left its mad gallop and dropped into a steady trot that she could more easily keep on terms with. The water was still well over her knees, but did not seem to be getting any deeper, and the cow thrashed its way steadily through it.

She had begun to hope now, and could think more clearly. She wondered what would happen when they came to a fence, and almost at once they came to one. Two posts, set a dozen feet apart, loomed suddenly out of the darkness, and the cow went straight between them. It was only when they were through that she realised that it must be some sort of gate, and that the gate was open, and then she thought that if this one was open, perhaps others would be, and the cow would know where to find them. For a moment she felt a sense of triumph, and then, perhaps because she had let her concentration waver, she lost her footing and fell. She fell full length in the water, so that for a moment even her face went under, and still the cow dragged her forward, with her feet in their heavy, water-logged boots trailing behind her. She screamed, and choked, and screamed again, and either her scream or her sheer dead weight checked the animal's way for a moment. Just for a moment it hesitated, and with a last effort of the will she doubled her legs under her and got to her feet again. She was wet all through now. Her sodden clothes dragged at her, and she choked as she breathed with the water she had swallowed, but still she had not let go of the rope, and when the cow went forward again, again she went with it.

Time, which had been her own, meant nothing to her now. The animal and she went on together, bent solely on the business of staying alive. They passed more gates, and then there was a moment when she found, even in her exhaustion, that she was moving more freely, and knew, without daring to look, that the level of the water had fallen till it was hardly over her ankles. The pace slackened, too. The cow was no longer driven by fear, but going steadily where it wanted to go. Then, quite suddenly, the water ended, and they were on dry land. It was some sort of a roughly paved track, and there was a low wall on one side of them. Then another wall closed in on the other side of them, and now for the first time they came to a gate that was shut. It was a heavy wooden gate, barring their way between the two walls on either hand, and the cow stopped at it, peering through the bars of the gate into the darkness beyond. Then at last Helen eased the loop of rope from off her arm, because she no longer had any need of it. She threw the looped end of the rope over the beast's neck, so that it would not catch its feet in it, and was going forward to open the gate when the cow lifted its head and bellowed. It was quite a different sound now, deeper and not so long drawn, an ordinary cow's moo, though to Helen it sounded full of relief and thankfulness, perhaps even of triumph. She pushed past the animal's wet flank and fumbled with the fastenings of the gate, and then, barely a dozen yards ahead, a light opened suddenly out of the darkness. It was a door that had opened, a door with a light inside it, and there was a figure, silhouetted against the light, standing in the doorway. The gate came open under her hand, and she swung it back. The cow and she went through together, and the figure ahead left the doorway and came forward to meet them.

She had known who it was the moment the door opened, but now that they were face to face, she did not know what to say to him. They stood there, facing each other across the cow's back in the yellow light of the doorway, and still neither of them spoke. Then he sighed, a sigh that seemed to come out of the depth of his body. "You," he said. "You of all people. What are you doing here?"

There was too much to explain, and she did not feel up to explanations. She set her mind to work, but the words that came out were basic. She said, "The cow was tied to a post, and I let it go. Is it yours?"

"She's my best milker," he said. "And you saved her from the river." He was silent for a moment, and then said again, "You of all people."

"She saved me," said Helen. She looked up at him in desperation, as if she had done something wrong. "I saved her, and then she saved me. We saved each other."

He sighed again, and then nodded. "Go into the house," he said. "I won't be a minute. I'll just see to her." He picked up the rope hanging across the cow's neck and went off with it across the yard, and Helen went into the house. She was in a farm kitchen, or she supposed it was the kitchen. It was lit by a single oil lamp standing on the table, and it smelt, the whole house smelt, like all the farmhouses she could ever remember and like none of the houses she had ever lived in, an unrefined smell, but oddly sweet and, above all, old. Nothing would ever change that smell, not whatever you did, as long as the house stood, and in any case she did not want it changed. Her panic and desperation had died out of her, and she felt utterly at peace, as if time was her own again. There was a coal fire burning in an open grate, and she went and stood by it, with her hands on the mantel shelf above it and her head hanging, while the water dripped off her clothes and dried out, almost as she watched it, on the warm flagstones under her feet. Then she heard the door shut and turned and found him standing just inside the door, looking at her.

He said, "You're wet, you're wet through," but he did not ask her how it had happened. He thought for a moment. "You'll have to change your clothes," he said. "I can't take you home yet. The water's over the road. It won't be very long, but we can't go yet. Wait here, and I'll find you something."

The stairs led straight up out of the room, and he went up them. She turned to the fire again, hearing him moving about upstairs, and not caring what he was doing or how long it took. Presently he came half-way down the stairs and called to her. He said, "You can come up now," and she left the fire and went up the stairs after him. The landing at the top was dark, but there was a door open half-way along, with the same soft yellow light shining out of it. He went on ahead of her. "The electricity's gone," he said. "There's been a lot of rain up-country, and there must be a power-line down." When he reached the door he stood aside, and she went into the room ahead of him.

It was a bedroom, with a bed in one corner covered with a white cotton counterpane. There was a big wardrobe and a chest-of-drawers with an oil lamp burning on it, and nothing else in the room. A wood fire burned fiercely in the grate, adding a red flicker to the steady yellow glow of the lamp. It must have been laid with dry wood and kindling to catch as quickly as that. There were some clothes laid on the counterpane of the bed, but she could not see what they were. She was looking at the photographs round the walls, portraits and groups, with clothes that she could see, even from where she was, went back over several generations to the beginning of photography, the portrait gallery of a class that did not hire fashionable painters. There were even some beasts, horses and cows, and what looked like a dog.

He followed her into the room, and for a moment they stood there looking at each other. His face was drawn, his dark eyes very wide. Then he turned and went out, shutting the door behind him.

She went to the fire and stood by it till its heat got through to her, and then she began to take off her wet clothes. She still had not looked at the clothes on the bed. Nothing worried her at all. She took off all her clothes and stood in front of the fire again, turning herself and moving her arms and legs slowly, so that the warmth dried every inch of her skin. When she was perfectly dry and warm, she went over and looked at the clothes on the bed. There was a tweed skirt, very plain but presentable, and of what looked very much the right size and length. There was a cotton shirt, a man's shirt, which would be much too big for her, but she could tuck it into the skirt, and a plain dark jersey. She left them and went back to the fire again, and then the door opened and Matthew Summers came in and shut the door behind him. He was wearing only a shirt and trousers, and looked all hard length.

She did not do any of the conventional things she should have done, like ordering him out of the room or catching up clothes to cover herself. She did not say anything at all. Only her arms came up by instinct, one arm covering her breasts and the other hand her mount of Venus, and so, in the classic pose of the goddess surprised bathing, she stood in the glow of the fire and looked at him as he came towards her. She was helpless anyhow, but did not even pretend to herself that it was the helplessness of her circumstances that held her. The helplessness was within her. She was experiencing what she had never experienced before, and would not have believed she could experience, an immediate, shattering physical attraction to the man in front of her, so that as he came across to her, her head fell back, and her lips parted a little, and she all but held out her arms to him. She did not hold them out, but he came and took her gently by the wrists and spread her arms wide and stood there with his eyes going slowly over the whole of her body.

He said, "Oh my God, but you're lovely" in a voice so deep that it was almost a rumble. He pushed her back, still gently, towards the bed, so that she first sat on it and then lay back on the cotton counterpane, while he swept the waiting clothes off the bed with one hand and began undoing his own with the other. He had none of Steve's boudoir tricks, but she did not need them. She was ready, even shamefully ready, for him before he came to her, and when he did, she was engulfed in waves of an appalling, unimaginable pleasure that blotted out all thought and all time.

When he got up from the bed, he dragged the bedclothes, counterpane and all, down from under her to her feet, and then up again over her, covering her to the neck as she lay with her face on the pillow, looking up at him. He said, "Sleep now. You'll need your sleep. I'll call you when the road's clear." She moved her head on the pillow but did not say anything. He gathered up the clothes she was to wear and put them once more across the foot of the bed. Then he went across and put more wood on the fire. Finally he picked up his own clothes in one hand and her wet things in the other, and went out of the door with them, shutting it behind him. Time, infinite time, was her own again, and she shut her eyes and went to sleep at once.

She woke when he came into the room, but he must have come in at other times while she was asleep, because the fire still burnt as high as ever. Now he said, "You'd best get up and dress. We can go now."

She said, "All right," and he turned and went out of the room again. She wanted her privacy now, because she did not want him to see her getting into the borrowed, perhaps awkward clothes, but in fact they were not awkward at all. The shirt, when she put it over her head, hung on her like a man's nightshirt, but the skirt fitted her almost perfectly, and she tucked all the length of shirt down inside it, making up for the underclothes she had not got. Then she put on the jersey, tucking up the shirt sleeves under the jersey sleeves, and then turning the jersey sleeves back to her wrists. She felt perfectly warm and comfortable, only she had nothing on her feet, and she went out of the room and along the landing and down the stairs barefoot.

He was waiting for her in the kitchen. He said, "That's right," with a sort of general approval, as if she were a child who had done what it was told. Her gumboots were standing by the fire, and the rest of her clothes were tied in a bundle on the table. He picked up the boots and brought them over to her. "You'd best put them on," he said. "They'll be a bit damp still, but it's the best we can do, and you won't have to wear them long. Your clothes are still too damp to wear."

She said again, "All right." She put her bare feet into the boots. They were still warm now from the fire, but she could feel the damp in them, and they would strike cold presently. Then he picked up the bundle of clothes, and they went out into the yard. There was a Land-Rover standing outside the door. He helped her into the near-side seat and went round and got in on the other side. He started the engine and switched the lights on, and the car moved off. The night was pitch dark, and she could see nothing but what the headlights picked out in front of them. They went through a couple of gates, already standing open, and then there was the road ahead, dipping slightly towards the lower ground that she knew lay between them and the village. After a bit there was water on the road, and they went through it slowly, but it did not seem very deep and did not last very long.

Ladon, when they came to it, was all asleep, without a light showing anywhere, and the roads were dry. It still had not rained here, and the river had come nowhere near the village. He turned right at the crossroads, and a minute later the village was behind them and only Spandles in front.

He stopped when they came to the drive, and for the first time he spoke. "I won't turn in," he said. "Someone might see the lights. Can you walk from here?"

She said, "Of course," and they both got out, and he handed her her bundle of clothes, and then neither of them seemed to know what to do. Finally it was she who moved. She went up to him and put out a hand and just touched one of his hands. "Thank you," she said, but he shook his head and sighed and got back into the car again, and she set off along the drive. When she got to the back door, she turned and could just see the lights of the car heading back towards Ladon.

The lights were on again when she put down the switch inside the back door. She put her bundle of damp clothes on the kitchen table. She could deal with them in the morning. Then she went straight upstairs and dropped her borrowed clothes on the floor and got into bed. The clock on the bedside table said just after eleven, but it was not an alarm-clock, and she had to be up in the morning to go and fetch Joan Winthrop. Helen did not generally need an alarm-clock. She willed herself to wake at seven, and a moment later she was asleep.

----◄◆►----

Chapter 11

She woke to the sound of someone coming upstairs. She thought at first it was Steve, and that she had overslept and not heard him get up. Then she remembered that Steve was away, and for a moment she panicked. She half sat up, staring at the door of the room, and then the door opened and Joan Winthrop put her head in and looked at her. She knew from the way she looked that she had looked in before, and found her asleep, and left her sleeping. Now she had that same small smile on her face, and when she pushed the door open and came in, Helen saw that she had a tray in her hand with tea-things on it. They were not the things she generally used in the morning, but they matched, and were nicely set out, and looked inviting. She could not remember when she had last eaten or drunk anything, and she knew she needed the tea desperately.

She said, "Oh I'm so sorry. I must have overslept." It did not mean anything, because she obviously had overslept, but she was still not fully awake, and said the words that came to her.

Joan put the tray down on the bedside table. "I expect you were in late," she said. "I came over in the evening, as a matter of fact, to see if you were all right when the lights went, and found you were out." She stood for a moment looking down at her, still smiling that small, curiously wistful smile. Then she stooped and picked up the tweed skirt from the floor, where Helen had dropped it the night before.

Helen said, "No, leave that. I'll—" but Joan shook her head and went to the door, still carrying the skirt.

"I'll take it," she said. "It's mine, anyway. You'd better put the other things away somewhere." Then she went out and shut the door quietly behind her.

Helen stared at the shut door, listening to Joan's footsteps going steadily down the stairs. After a bit she got out of bed and went to the wardrobe and got her dressing-gown and put it on. As she came back across the room, she stooped and picked up the shirt and jersey, and then stood wondering where to put them. She had to put them away, as Joan had said. It was no good being defiant about it. Faced suddenly with apparently total catastrophe, she could only do the next thing under her hand, and this was it. She folded the shirt and jersey neatly on the bed and put them away at the bottom of a drawer, under her own neatly-folded woollies. With the jersey on top of the shirt, they were immediately invisible, and in any case the possibility that Steve would ever look in the bottom of the drawer was so remote as to be ridiculous. Then she went back to the bed and sat on it and started to pour out the tea. That also was the next thing under her hand, and her physical need for it was absolute. Some time, presently, she had to think, but she could not think until she had something in her stomach. She even put a spoonful of sugar in her cup, because Joan had put sugar on the tray. Helen never drank sugar in her tea, but there it was, on the tray, and she needed it.

She drank three cups, very hot and two of them sweet, sitting there on the side of the bed and listening to Joan being busy downstairs. No constructive thought of any kind came into Helen's head. She made no decisions beyond the scope of the tea-tray, because she could not see that there was anything left for her to decide. She seemed to be completely at the mercy of circumstances and other people, almost as if she were a child again, upstairs here alone in her bedroom while things were being arranged for her downstairs. Only her body was not a child's body, and somewhere inside her body there was a seeping well-spring of pleasure and excitement untouched and unaffected by the stunned speculations of her mind. What had happened the night before seemed as remote from reality as a dream, but, like some dreams, it coloured, at least for the time, her whole apprehension of reality. She sat there, already comforted and stabilised by the tea, but in a state of compulsive inertia, until she heard Joan coming upstairs again. Then she put her cup back on the tray and got up, belting her dressing-gown more tightly round her, and picked up the tray and went to the door with it.

She opened it, holding the tray in one hand, and met Joan in the doorway. Joan said, "I'll take that, shall I?" and held out her hands for the tray.

Helen put the tray into them. "Oh—yes," she said, "thank you, I needed that." They smiled at each other with a sort of hesitant confidentiality, which Helen could not reject and, having accepted it, found not unwelcome.

Joan said, "When will your husband be back?" She said "your husband," not "Mr. Anderson," as an ordinary woman from the village would have done.

"This evening. I don't know exactly at what time, but this evening."

Joan nodded. "I knew he'd gone," she said. "And then this morning I saw his car was still out. But I didn't know when he'd be back." There were limits even to Ladon's knowledge. "Well, you get yourself dressed," she said, "and I'll do a bit more downstairs. And then perhaps you'd run me back."

Helen said, "Of course. I'm sorry—I never thought. How did you get here?"

"Oh I walked. When I found you didn't come. I thought I'd better."

Helen said again, "I'm sorry—" but Joan cut her off.

"Oh that's all right," she said. "I like walking. But it had better be in your time, and that doesn't give me much longer." She turned and took the tray downstairs. For a moment Helen watched her go. Then she went back into her room and set about getting dressed.

When she went downstairs, the marks of Joan's activities were everywhere. Steve would not notice them, though beyond a certain point he would have noticed their absence. She herself saw them, not because she was houseproud, but because they represented things she would otherwise have had to do herself, and did not take much pleasure in doing. When the system became established, the whole house would look and feel different, and then she would get positive pleasure out of it. At the moment it was Joan herself who mattered, not the housework she had done and would do. She was in the kitchen, still doing things, but ready to go. She said, "I put your things to dry. You'll be able to put them away by tea-time." As she had with the things upstairs, she meant put them away where Steve would not see them, and took the need as a matter of course. At a blow, Helen's precarious confidentiality with Steve as against the world had been replaced by a new confidentiality with Joan as against Steve. She knew it ought to have shocked her, but was conscious of an unexamined sense of relief, because Joan was a real person. Joan said, "What happened to you, to get wet through like that?" It was only the second question she had asked. Everything else she had taken for granted.

Helen said, "I got caught in the flood-water. I was walking by the river."

"And the river drove you to Calton?"

Helen nodded. "That's right," she said. She could not bring herself to mention the cow. That would have sounded ridiculous, and it had not been ridiculous at all.

To her surprise, Joan laughed. She said, "Mr. Summers and his river." She called him "Mr. Summers"—that was the extraordinary thing. She had called Steve "your husband," but she called Matthew Summers "Mr. Summers." She said,

"Well, I'm glad you brought my skirt back. It might have been awkward getting it back now." She had the skirt neatly parcelled in paper on the table, and now she took off her overall and put it along with the parcelled skirt into the bag she had brought with her. She put the parcel underneath the overall, at the bottom of the bag. She was putting things away too.

After that they dealt entirely in conventionalities. They fixed Joan's next day and Helen paid her what she owed her. She still had not heard from Celia what this should be, but Joan told her and she paid. It was all perfectly friendly. It was only when they were in the car and half-way back to the village that Helen asked the question that was somehow uppermost in her mind. She said, "Does your husband know?" She kept her eyes on the road, as Joan had when she had driven her back to Spandles.

Joan said, "Not to say knows. He knows, of course. He'd be bound to. But there's nothing he can tell himself."

Helen said, "Why would he be bound to?" She was thinking of Steve, who would be back in the evening.

"Well, Jack's like that. Always on the look-out for anything against him, whether it's there or not. It needn't be the same with you. Your husband's not like that."

Helen said, "But you haven't met him, have you?"

"No," said Joan, "but I've heard. And Jack's met him, of course, at the garage. He didn't like him much. He wouldn't, of course. They're very different."

"Different how?" said Helen. This was something she had to understand.

"Well, what I said. Jack's always expecting someone to do him down. Including with me, I mean. He always has, right from the time we were married. Not jealous, exactly. Just expecting the worst. And the fact that we hadn't any children made it worse. He knew I wanted them. But your husband isn't like that. It would never occur to him for a moment that anything like this could happen. Especially with Mr.

Summers. It's funny, really." She laughed her small, quiet laugh, and in a corner of her new, stunned mind Helen could see it was funny, too, and half smiled at it, because she knew that Joan also had her eyes on the road and would not see the smile.

She said, "What about you?"

"Oh that'll be over now. But I wouldn't have missed it for the world."

Helen said, "I'm sorry." It seemed the natural thing to say, as if she had got a book out of the library that Joan had been waiting for.

"Oh well, I was expecting it. As soon as I saw you."

This time Helen really was shocked. She had not expected anything ever to shock her again, but this shocked her. "You were expecting it?" she said.

"Oh yes. He'd be bound to want you, looking like you do, and if he wanted you, he'd have you. I knew that. But don't worry about me. I mean, I don't love him or anything like that. And it'll make life that much easier. It's been a bit difficult at times. It'll be easier for you, living where you are."

Helen said, "But I don't want—" but Joan cut her off, as she had earlier in the morning.

"You will," she said. "You'll find you will, whatever you think. But don't go falling in love with him. He won't be in love with you." She was silent for a moment. "At least," she said, "I hope he won't. That might make real trouble. But I don't think he can. He's not like that. But don't you."

Helen said, "All right," meekly, as if an elder sister had told her not to eat too many sweets, and then they were back at the garage. Helen stopped outside the bungalow, and they were back to conventionalities again.

She had shopping to do, but could not think of it now. She had to be alone for a bit, and this evening Steve would be back. She turned the car and drove slowly back to Spandles. If Joan had expected it, and Jack had in some fashion known about Joan, Jack would be expecting it too. And she remembered the way he had looked at her, with that sort of inward amusement, and she knew that he had expected it, and would be pleased, because he knew about Joan, and did not like Steve. For all she knew, half Ladon might be expecting it, being the village it was. Half Ladon would be looking at her speculatively, and for all she knew with a pleasurable speculation, because they probably did not like Steve either. But she must give them nothing to speculate about. Nobody except Joan could possibly know what had happened last night, and there would be nothing more for them to know, whatever Joan said. It was then she thought of Charles, and the way he had questioned her about Matthew Summers, and the way Celia had looked at him, and the curious silence between them. Surely not Celia too? And yet why not, with Charles the way he was, and Celia coming and going always on her own? Only with Celia no one would ever know, not even Charles, because with Charles there would be only his mind to tell him, and in a thing like this the mind was less knowledgeable. She gave it up. The thing was too much for her altogether.

When she got in, she again did automatically the next thing under her hand. She put her boots, still standing damp in the passage where she had left them, to dry in the kitchen, and found her other things where Joan had put them to dry. She washed out her under-things and pressed her skirt and jersey and put them away upstairs, and then set herself to think what she had to do, on an ordinary day, with Steve coming home in the evening. Beyond making the bed, there was nothing to do in the house, because Joan had done what was immediately necessary. One of the things she had to do was shop, and that meant facing the village. For a moment she thought of driving into Skrene, but that was nonsense. All she had to do could be done in the village, and she could not avoid the village indefinitely. Come to that, if she did avoid it, the village would probably put its

own construction on it. What she must do is behave exactly as she normally did.

The trouble was that her normality had changed. She had
become in many ways a different person overnight, and
what still shook her was less the change itself than the ease
with which it had been accomplished, and the fact that, on
balance, for all the complications, she was enjoying it. The
truth must be that the pressure for change had been building up for some time, above all in her relations with Steve,
and that Matthew Summers had done no more than release
it. She remembered him with enormous pleasure and a curious kind of affection, but her heart did not go out to him as
a person, perhaps because he did not want it and had not
asked for it. Joan's attitude, which had seemed so shatter-
ingly matter-of-fact at the time, was more intelligible to her
now, and Joan's warning, though perfectly correct and well
judged, had not really been needed. She was not in love
with Matthew Summers, and was not likely to be. Especially, she reminded herself, when there was in any case to
be nothing more between them. She supposed she had in
some way grown up, very suddenly and painlessly, but with
the characteristic mixture of exhilaration and apprehension
that growing up usually entailed. What she had to do now
was to ensure that the change in her was not too immediately apparent, because that would set people wondering
what had produced it, and she did not want them to know.
Meanwhile her new self, clad in the guise of her old self,
must go shopping in Ladon.

The one person she did not want to meet there was Celia,
because with Celia there must be a double complication.
Celia might be speculating about her—she thought she already was—just as Joan had speculated, but she herself was
now speculating about Celia. Her own speculation, which
was part of the change in her, might show, and provide
fresh fuel for Celia's speculation about her. Her new relation
with Joan was governed by the fact that Joan had known, or

taken for granted, everything about her from the start, and
had concealed nothing about herself. But Celia was
different from Joan in every way, almost her opposite. Concealment was second nature to her. Between herself and
Celia there could be no knowledge, and certainly nothing, at
least on her side, could be taken for granted. Between them
there could only be speculation, and the speculation would
overshadow their relations as much as their mutual knowledge illuminated her relations with Joan. It was Joan who
was her friend now, and even this new friendship must be
concealed, at least for the moment, from Celia. Luckily, as
she would now be seeing Joan regularly, her friendship with
her would in due course acquire an innocent explanation,
but it must be allowed to appear gradually if it was not to be
suspect. It occurred to her, curiously, that now she would
prefer to meet Celia in Steve's company, whereas before she
had always felt the opposite.

She made her plans for supper—she assumed Steve would
be back for supper—and made out a shopping list, as she always did, on the back of an envelope, and got the car out
and drove to the village. She did everything exactly as she
always did, only now she was consciously playing a part,
whereas before she had been playing it natural. She did not
in fact find it difficult, and was pleased by the way she was
carrying it off. If she was carrying it off. Ladon being
Ladon, she could not be sure of this, but she thought she
was. She had a more difficult performance ahead of her in
the evening. Steve was an easier audience than Ladon, but
on her side the performance would be more difficult. He
would come home, and probably bring her some small present from London, and tell her about his business there, and
make routine enquiries about affairs at home during his absence. They would have supper, and go to bed, and he
would make love to her. He always made love to her when
he came home after being away, partly, she supposed, be-

cause he wanted to, but also, she suspected, because he felt in some way it was the proper thing to do.

That would be the crunch. That was the one thing, she knew, that was irretrievably altered, and she did not, now, trust her body as she trusted her mind. She finished her shopping, and went home, and did what she had to do in the kitchen. Then she went out for a walk, walking eastwards instead of westwards and keeping far from the river. When she got back from her walk, she tidied herself up, making herself, quite consciously, look as nice as possible, and sat down to await Steve's return.

Chapter 12

For the second time in two days, she woke to hear someone coming upstairs, but this time she knew it was Steve. She had overslept again, but when she had gone to sleep, Steve had been with her. She lay there, staring at the door, not in a panic now, but keeping a tight hold on herself. When he came in, he carried a cup of tea for her, not a complete tea-tray, as Joan had done, but a single cup, because he had made tea for himself in the kitchen and was sparing her a cup of it. He smiled at her cheerfully. She knew at once that he was feeling pleased with himself, and was conscious of an enormous relief. Joan had been perfectly right about him. He must have noticed something, because she knew there had been things to notice, but instead of looking elsewhere for a reason, he had simply taken the credit to himself. That made him pleased with himself, and pleased with her in a rather proprietary sort of way, as he had used to be when they were first married. She had known women who claimed that having an affair improved their relations with their husbands, but she had not believed them, and had in any case assumed that she herself would not have one. Now here it was, and once more, as she had in her new relation with Joan, she felt shocked less by the change in itself than by the ease with which it had come about.

Steve said, "You've overslept. You were still sleeping like the dead when I got up. I didn't want to disturb you." He was pleased with himself for that, too. He glowed with the double warmth of present domestic virtue and remembered

marital prowess. He put the cup on the bedside table, and
she smiled at him cosily, considering him from her new-
found privacy with complete detachment. A lot of women
would have jumped at him, even without the needs that had
led her to marry him. There was nothing wrong with him
except this intrinsic inability to get himself taken seriously.

She said, "I'm so sorry. You're quite right. I did sleep like
the dead. But I'll get up now. Just let me drink my tea, and
I'll be up and get breakfast. Will you be working today?"

He was at the door already on his way out, and now he
stopped for a moment with one hand on the door-handle,
looking back at her. "I've already started," he said, but in
his present mood even that was a source of satisfaction to
him. "I'm going to work all day today and go fishing tomorrow." He smiled at her again and went out, shutting the
door behind him. Helen dropped back onto her pillow and
felt the relief drain out of her. She could not prevent his
going fishing, and could not even give herself a good reason
why she should want to. She only knew that if he went
fishing, he would be on Calton ground, and she did not want
him to have anything to do with Calton. She knew there
were several strands to this wish, some of them probably
mutually contradictory, but she could not sort them out
now. She knew he would go, and the last thing she could do
was try to stop him. She was full of an ill-defined apprehension, but consciously helpless. By the time she reached
for her tea, it was almost cold, but perhaps it had not been
very hot in the first place. She drank it nevertheless, and
then set about getting up. She found herself wishing, of all
things, that Joan was coming today, but she was not due
until tomorrow.

Steve was still cheerful over breakfast. His news from
London had been good, and this had given him a fresh en-
thusiasm for his work. She wondered, not for the first time,
whether it was his success that he took seriously rather than
his actual writing. She thought it would be a sign of grace in

him if this was so, but the trouble was that he would never admit it. He wanted other people to take his work seriously, and he did not discuss it with her precisely because, with his keen defensive instincts, he sensed that she did not. The people he met in London, his agents and publishers in particular, would at least pretend to take it seriously, because it was in their own interests to do so, and the pretence, if it was a pretence, would be a natural part of their professional manner with him. But the business side of his London visit he had already discussed with her when he had got home the evening before. Today his excitement had switched to the book he was now working on, and there was nothing there to involve her. At least it would keep him occupied and preoccupied all day. It would also probably, she thought, keep him working late tonight, so that she could be safely asleep by the time he came to bed.

Tomorrow morning would bring Joan. He had not remembered this, and she did not mention it. She would be glad to have Joan, and she was even conscious of a mildly amused speculation how they would get on when they met, but she did not want to have to talk to him about Joan until after they actually had met. Then it would be his reaction to her that they would talk about, and that was safe ground. The idea that she herself could have any private relation with Joan would not occur to him. Tomorrow morning he would be working, and she could talk to Joan in privacy downstairs. Tomorrow morning was safe enough. It was the afternoon that worried her. In the afternoon Joan would be gone, and he would go fishing. Meanwhile she had today to herself.

Even next day she did not mention Joan until she was ready to go and fetch her. Steve was already at work then, and she went up and put her head in the door of his room. "I'm just going to fetch Joan Winthrop," she said. "Shan't be long."

He looked up. Sometimes when she interrupted him he

went out of his way to lift his head slowly and look at her in a slightly abstracted way. It was a part of the act she had come to recognise, perhaps even a hardly conscious one, but part of the act all the same. But today he looked up sharply enough, and she had all his attention. "What, pretty Joan?" he said. "Good Lord, I'd forgotten. All right, off you go." He was starting to look abstracted now, but his pleasurable interest had been unmistakable. She thought he would be down to make his number with pretty Joan when she arrived. She nodded and shut the door quietly and went downstairs.

Joan was waiting for her, and came out of the house as soon as the car turned into the yard. She had her bag in her hand, but this time she would take home in it nothing more than she had brought. She did not mention that today Helen had not overslept, but Helen was conscious of a small, unspoken joke between them. For Helen it was a double joke, because she had overslept the day before as well. That was a part of the joke she thought Joan would appreciate, but she did not propose to admit her to it. Joan said, "Your husband got back all right?"

It was a comprehensive question, but passable as the merest formality, and Helen did not answer it comprehensively, nor did Joan expect her to. Already they were talking in shorthand. Helen said, "Yes, thank you," but she said it cheerfully and with assurance, and Joan was satisfied.

She said, "That's good," and for the rest of the short drive they sat side by side in companionable silence. Helen left her car standing outside the back door. She would need it presently to take Joan home, and Steve would not be taking his out today. They went into the house together. Joan got her working overall out and hung her bag on a hook on the kitchen door. They were still discussing what needed to be done when the door opened and Steve came in, speaking to Helen as he came.

He said, "Look, if you're going into the village—" and

then broke off. "Good Lord," he said, "you're back already. Good morning, Mrs. Winthrop. How nice to see you. And how kind of you to come and help us." He went across to Joan with his hand outstretched and his eyes crinkled with pleasure. She watched the now familiar gambit with a small, slightly malicious amusement, but it was Joan she was watching, not Steve. Joan put her hand out to him pleasantly enough, but the arm was held straight, keeping her distance, and her eyes were very slightly closed. She smiled, of course, in response to his smile, but to Helen there was as much amusement in the smile as there was pleasure. Once again she and Joan were sharing a small joke at Steve's expense, but she could trust Joan not to let him feel it. For the matter of that, she could trust him not to feel it.

Joan said, "Oh it's a pleasure," and took her hand away.

For a moment there was silence, and it was Helen who broke it, because she did not want it to show. She said, "Was there something you wanted in the village?" and Steve came back into the act.

"Well yes," he said, "but it's not urgent. Only tobacco. The usual. They've got it at Mallet's."

Helen said, "Of course. I'll be taking Joan back presently, and I'll get it then, if that will be all right." She said "Joan," not "Mrs. Winthrop," as he had done, because it was natural enough, nowadays, that she should call the daily by her Christian name, especially a woman as young as Joan, and there was no harm in letting their friendly relation appear from the start, especially when this was Joan's second day. She thought she could trust Joan, if she needed to refer to her, to call her "Mrs. Anderson" in talking to Steve, at least for the present.

Steve said, "That'll be fine." He looked at the two of them, smiling comprehensively, and then pulled himself up with a start, mentally, thought Helen, squaring his shoulders, though she had never seen anyone actually do it. "Well," he said, "I must get back to the grindstone." Then he smiled again, this time at Joan, and turned and went out.

They stood for a moment in silence, hearing him go back upstairs. Then Joan spoke, stepping right back into complete confidentiality, and with an uncanny echo of Helen's own thought of the morning before. She said, "You might do a lot worse, you know. There's many women would be glad to do as well. And there's the money, too. You'll want to watch what you're doing. He wouldn't stand for much, not if you hurt his vanity." She smiled suddenly in the way she had, letting her softness show, but still quite uncompromising. "What you've really got to do," she said, "is make up your mind what you want. Otherwise you're going to have things decided for you, like I expect they always have been. And you shouldn't, not with those looks."

Helen sat suddenly on the edge of the kitchen table. She was not conscious of any real physical weakness, but she desperately needed support, and even the kitchen table was better than nothing. She looked at Joan despairingly. "I'm lonely," she said. As so often with her, the words came before the conscious thought, but once they were spoken, she knew that that was what she had been thinking.

Joan nodded. "I dare say you are," she said. "I can understand that. So's he, only he keeps himself like that, and keeps you lonely doing it. So am I, for that matter, only I'm better built for it than you are, for all my pretty ways. So are a lot of people. So's that Mrs. Fearon. But then she always would have been, even without his accident. I reckon she was born lonely, that one. And he's not, that's the funny thing. Stuck in that chair all the time, and never lonely. It's the way you're made, really. Only you're not made that way. You could be lonelier than you are, all the same."

"I have been," said Helen. "That was why I married."

Joan nodded. "There you are, then," she said. Then she caught herself up and unmistakably squared her shoulders. "Well," she said, "back to the grindstone, or he'll be wondering what I'm doing here." She smiled at Helen, who for all her desolation smiled back. Then she gathered up her gear and went out, as they had agreed she should, to start on the stairs.

Helen got up off the table and started doing things in the kitchen, but she moved slowly, and her mind was not on what she was doing. It was all very well for Joan to say she must make up her mind, but what in fact were the alternatives open to her? It was even all very well for her to say she was lonely, but what sort of companionship did she want, and with whom? Even with what sort of person? She wondered in her despair whether she did not perhaps have the worst of both worlds, whether she was not at the same time doomed to loneliness and incapable of living with it. She envied Joan's disenchanted independence, but certainly not her life with Jack in the bungalow. In a way she even envied Celia's life with Charles, wheel-chair and all—at least, she thought, Celia was needed—but not her pathological privacy. Celia was not happy, as in some almost unintelligible but admirable way Joan was. She might have shared her newly-discovered desolation with Celia. She thought now that this was what had instinctively drawn her to Celia when they had first met. But Celia could not share her desolation with anyone, and already this incapacity of confidence had come between them. She could in some degree share in Joan's happiness, and had an almost desperate need to do so. She was already dependent on Joan in a way she could not have believed possible only a few days ago. But that was no more than an alleviation of her enduring need. She did not want an amused cheerfulness, she wanted warmth and peace. She knew where she had last felt warmth and peace, and how it had shattered her defences, but there was no way out there—at least if Joan was right, and Joan ought to know.

She finished what she had to do in the kitchen, and knew that Joan would do whatever was immediately needed in the rest of the house. She had an urge to go and talk to her again, but she could not stand by talking while Joan worked, especially not on the stairs, where Steve would hear at least the sound of their voices. The best thing she could do was go out for a walk, which always settled her mind, but there would be Steve coming down for coffee and conversation at eleven, and she could not leave Joan to cope with him. Then she thought, well, why not? Joan would not mind, if she warned her, and Steve would positively enjoy it. She went out of the kitchen into the hall, where Joan was busy on her knees half-way up the stairs, and spoke to her quietly through the banisters. She said, "Look, I'm going out for a walk. I shan't be long, only Steve will be coming down for his coffee at about eleven. Will that be all right?"

Joan put her face to the banisters and smiled down at her. "I'll manage," she said. "You go on out. Only don't walk too far. Apart from anything else, you've got to take me home at twelve. And get his tobacco."

"I shan't," said Helen. "I'll be back long before then."

Joan nodded. "All right," she said. "It'll do you good. I know it does me."

Helen said, "Yes," and went through into the back of the house to get her things. It was while she was putting them on that she realised that she had spoken of Steve as "Steve" when she had been talking to Joan. But then what else could she have called him? "Mr. Anderson" was far outside their present degree of familiarity, and "my husband" would have sounded absurdly stilted. It was all nonsense, anyway. She tied on her headscarf and went out of the back door into the yard.

It was grey weather again, and dead quiet, with only the faintest breeze blowing from the west. She went along the garden and down the steps into the fields. For a moment she hesitated. Then she set her face due south towards the river. It was time she had a good straight look at it, and there was nothing to be afraid of today. There had been no rain for days, and farther westwards the cattle were on the fields.

It would not take long, walking briskly and going straight down to it like this. It was down, too. She had not realised before how much the land fell. The slope was gradual and dead flat, but very steady. There must be a considerable difference in height between the line of the road and the actual bank of the river. By the time the water was well over the fields, there would be a good six feet of water over the bank. She thought of her struggle with the tethered cow, and shivered suddenly. But today, and from here, you could not see the water at all. All the same, she meant to see it, and she went steadily on.

She climbed through the last fence and went cautiously forward. She could see the edge of the bank clearly in the grey light, but she still could not see the water. A few yards from the lip she hesitated. Then she turned and looked back at the house. She thought if there had been anyone in any of the front windows, she could have seen them, but there was no one. She got down on her hands and knees and crawled towards the lip, stealthily, as if she were stalking an enemy.

When she came to it, she stopped and, keeping her weight well back, craned forward and looked over. She saw at once that she need not have worried. The bank was not undercut here, though she thought she could see, downstream, places where it was. It fell in a slightly curved wall of mud, with a scatter of stones and roots showing from it here and there. She got to her feet, still hoping that her excess of caution had not been seen, and stood looking down from her full height on the face of the river.

The river took no notice of her. It ran steadily and with hardly a ripple between its enclosing walls. It carried nothing on its moving face, and it was difficult to tell how fast it was actually moving. She stooped and plucked a handful of grass and threw it outward onto the water. Even as she threw it, she remembered Matthew Summers' saying, "There's no need to throw things at it," but already she had thrown, and she was disconcerted to see how quickly the river carried the grass away. It was going much faster than she had thought, even at its present level. There was a suggestion of smooth power in it she did not at all like. She shivered again, stepped back a pace or two, and only then turned her back on it.

That was the Lod, Steve's Lod, and this afternoon he was going fishing in it. She shook herself, and started walking briskly back towards the house.

Chapter 13

She almost wondered whether she would find the coffee party still in progress, but there was silence in the kitchen as she took off her walking things, and when she went in, the coffee cups and all that went with them had been washed up and put away. Joan was evidently a believer in washing up as you go along, and Helen swore to herself that she would never in any circumstances yield to the temptation to leave the overnight washing-up for her to do in the morning. She knew that it would be, if only in Joan's subconscious mind, a small black mark against her, and she needed her approbation as she needed her cheerfulness. Meanwhile, she wanted coffee herself—it was not unreasonably late for it, and she had been walking. She put the kettle on and went out into the hall. She heard Joan moving about in the sitting room, which was where they had agreed she should be. Upstairs all was silence. She went and put her head in at the sitting-room door. "I'm back," she said. "Everything all right?"

Joan nodded. There was a small reminiscent smile on her face, but Helen felt a touch of constraint behind it. "Oh yes," she said, "fine. We had quite a talk. I'll tell you."

She turned to go on with her work, and Helen herself nodded and went back to the kitchen. They did not usually have much for lunch, and ate it at the kitchen table. It was only supper she laid in the dining room, to make it more of an occasion. She made her preparations for lunch, such as they were, and a little before twelve Joan came into the

kitchen and put her working things away. Then she took off
her overall and put it in the bag and Helen said "Ready?"
and Joan said "All ready" and they put their coats on and
went out into the yard. As if by agreement, they did not say
anything that mattered until they were out of the house.

Then Joan said, "Oh yes, quite a talk we had. I don't
know about the grindstone, but he didn't seem in any hurry
to get back upstairs."

Helen found herself suddenly anxious for a view of her
husband as seen through another woman's eyes, and an attractive woman at that. She had had the usual routine insin-
cerities in the small change of conversation, but never any
approach to a true picture. Attractive women did not generally tell other women the truth about their husbands. She
herself had met the wives of many of the buzzers and
droolers, but she never told them about the buzzing and
drooling. She did not think, to be honest, that this was so
much out of consideration for the wives' feelings as because
it was in some way against the rules of the game, even
though it was a game she herself had no particular wish to
get involved in. And now here was the attractive Joan, with
her almost painful candour and total disenchantment, and
Steve had evidently been putting his best foot forward with
her, and she longed to hear all about it. All the same, she
could not bring herself to ask a direct question. She merely
kept her eyes on the road and waited for Joan to go on.

Joan said, "He's got a lot of charm, you know. I mean,
real charm. Of course, a lot of it's routine. Well, you'll have
seen all that. Anyone with that amount of charm can't help
using it any more than he can help breathing. But there is
something appealing about him. I think it's because underneath he's so unsure of himself. He does the conquering
hero stuff, but all the time he's really asking for sympathy.
But of course, he couldn't do that to you, so you don't see it.
He's very young for his age, isn't he? Well, so are you in a
way, but it's a different way. You're what I'd call immature.

Or have been up to now. I don't think it's due to last much longer. But he's set that way, because he likes it, and he's found up to now it pays him. I expect that's where he gets his books from. Not that I've read any of them. It would take a terrible explosion to shake him out of it. I reckon you might provide it one of these days, too. Not because you're the person you are, almost in spite of it, but because you're his wife. He's put a lot of eggs in this one basket, and if you dropped the lot, he'd have an awful lot of unscrambling to do. It might be the making of him, at that. What it would do to you I don't know. You could blow yourselves apart, or you could both grow up and stay together. It might be worth trying, you know. I'm almost inclined to recommend it." She turned to Helen and smiled her sudden, disarming smile, and Helen took her eyes off the road for a moment and smiled back at her. "But of course recommending won't help, not with you. It'll happen or it won't happen, and you'll just find it has or it hasn't." She was quiet for a moment, looking ahead. They were almost into Ladon already. "I tell you one thing," she said. "I'm not making trouble telling you, because the trouble's already made. But you mustn't feel, if the thing blows up, that the guilt's all on your side. I should say, in a harmless sort of way, your husband's as promiscuous as a tom-cat. I mean—all innocent fun and no harm intended. But fair's fair, if the thing does blow up. Remember you start on level terms. Unless, I mean, there's been some commitment on your part, and I've already warned you against that."

The car turned into the yard and stopped outside the bungalow gate, but Joan did not make an immediate move to get out. She sat for a moment where she was, staring in front of her through the windscreen at a view that on any reckoning was almost totally devoid of interest. Then she said, "Look, have you got a minute? What I've been saying's all true enough, but it isn't really what I wanted to say."

Helen nodded. "I knew there was something," she said. "Go on."

Joan looked at her with interest. "Did you?" she said. "You're sharper than one gives you credit for. It's the help-less blonde act that takes one in. Well, that's good, because then you're more likely to take what I say seriously." She stopped a moment, once more looking ahead of her. Then she said, "He said he was going fishing in the river. I don't think that's a good thing. Can't you stop him?"

Everything inside Helen seemed suddenly to have stopped moving. For several seconds she did actually hold her breath. Then she shook her head. "I don't think so," she said. "Why?"

"Because I think it could be dangerous."

"The river really is dangerous, the river and the bank? I know it frightens me. I went down to look at it again just now, when I went out. I don't know why, but it scares me stiff."

Joan nodded. "I think you're right," she said. "But there's more to it than that. It's Mr. Summers' river, or he thinks it is."

Helen said, "But Steve got Mr. Summers' permission. He got it easily, too, at least by his account."

"I know," said Joan. "He told me. That's what frightens me."

Helen said, "Do you mean—" but Joan cut her short.

"I don't know," she said. "You must believe me, I don't know anything. I only know we don't want another Mr. Wetherby. Your husband's stepped too neatly into his shoes, and we don't want him going the same way." She opened the door on her side. "That's all," she said. "Now I must go, and so must you, or you'll be late for his lunch. But I had to tell you." She got out and stood for a moment holding the door open. "Do what you can," she said. Then she shut the door and was off to the gate. Helen sat for a moment, aware that her knees were shaking. Then she mastered herself and put the car in gear and turned it out onto the road again, heading back towards Spandles. Half-way home she remembered Steve's tobacco, but she did not believe he really needed it.

She drove fast and a little breathlessly. She did not yet know what she was going to do, but she was determined to do something. She left the car outside the door and almost ran into the house. She went into the hall and called "Steve! Steve!" up the stairs, but there was no reply. She knew what had happened as soon as she went into the kitchen and saw that half the lunch things had been used. There was a note on the table, but she did not stop to read it. She took off her coat and put on a mackintosh and boots. Her head was still covered. She started for the back door, and then turned back and took her walking-stick off one of the hooks on the wall. She needed it if she was in a hurry, and now she was in a hurry as she had never been before. She ran down the garden and stood for a moment at the top of the steps, looking westwards across the fields, hoping to see movement on the river-bank, but the day was darker than ever, and she could see nothing. A couple of fields away, well up from the river, a herd of cows grazed monumentally, but below them nothing moved. She gave what was almost a sob, hurried down the steps, and started running across the fields. She ran south-westwards, on a line that would bring her to the river well downstream from the house. After a bit she could run no longer, and dropped to a desperate walk, using the stick rhythmically to reinforce her suspect ankle. She kept an eye on the ground as far as she could, but most of the time she watched the line of the invisible river-bank, pushing her field of vision farther and farther downstream as she went westwards.

It must have been a quarter of an hour later that she suddenly saw him. He was still a long way ahead, but it was Steve, all right. The lower half of him was lost against the dark background, but she could see the movement of his arms as he cast methodically over the invisible water. Her relief poured out of her in a long sigh, and she changed course, aiming straight for him. She was going slower now, and already doubt and hesitation assailed her. She did not know what she was going to say to him when she got there, or even how she was going to account for her presence, which she felt instinctively would not be welcome, whether or not she found words for what she had to say. She wondered whether she might not simply watch him from a safe distance. He was so intent on his fishing that ten to one he would never notice her unless she came right up to him.

He was a lot nearer now, moving slowly downstream as he cast, but at nothing like her speed. She could see the whole of him quite clearly. She was not more than thirty or forty yards from him, and still closing with him, when the ankle let her down. She was so intent on watching him that she did not see the tussock of coarse grass that the cows had rejected, but it caught her foot and sent her sprawling. In her already great distress the fall disarmed her totally, but she knew she was not hurt. She lay for a moment as she had fallen, gasping on the damp grass. Then she recovered herself and got to her feet, and when she looked for him again, she could not see him.

For a moment she stopped dead, stunned and unable to believe her eyes, peering forward in the grey light as if she had somehow mislaid him. Then she began to run. She ran frantically now, ankle or no ankle, sobbing as she ran. When she was close enough, she began to scream, but she was so short of breath that there was not much power in her screams. She called, "Steve! Steve!" running now on a line parallel with the bank but always a few safe yards from that treacherous lip.

Nothing answered her. She turned and went as close to the edge as she dared, and looked down, but she could see nothing but the dark water. Then she ran on again, still screaming his name when she could find breath to scream with. After a bit she stopped and caught her breath, and called twice more with all the force of her lungs. For a moment she stood there listening in the enormous silence, and then she had her answer. It was a shout, rather faint and high-pitched, but a man's voice. It was still some way ahead of her. She ran on, very close to the bank now, and then she stopped and called again. The answer came at once, muffled by the bank, but much nearer now, and unbelievably a little behind her. She had come too far. She turned and ran back and called again, and this time the answering shout was almost at her feet. She dropped to her hands and knees, regardless of appearances now, and crawled to the edge of the bank, trailing the stick on the grass behind her. She reached the lip and peered over, and found a white, frightened face peering up into her own out of the dark water.

He was crouched at the foot of the bank, most of him in the river, with one hand clutching a projecting stone a foot up from the water. The other hand, as she saw in a moment of half-exasperation, still clutched his precious rod. The sling of his fishing-bag was still over his shoulder, but the bag itself floated on the water behind his back. There was no need now for explanations and no time for them. He said, "I'm all right, but I can't get up the damned bank. And the water's hellish cold."

She had not thought of this, and was almost glad she had not, though she should have. River-water was always colder than sea-water, and it did not, like the sea, hold its summer warmth after the autumn had set in. It came down from the cold hills, and was as cold as the hills it had come from. Even if a swimmer could keep afloat, the cold would get him sooner or later, just so long as he could not get out of the water. He said, "If I put the rod up, do you think you could give me a hand? I can kick a foot-hold in the bank, I think. I've got shoes on, not boots. But I must have something to hold onto."

She said, "I've got a stick." She pulled it out over the

bank and showed it to him, desperately anxious to give him all the reassurance she could.

"Oh God," he said, "that's marvellous. All right. I'll pass up the rod. Will you take it?" His precious rod, she thought, but she nodded.

"Pass it up," she said. He lifted it towards her gingerly, and she caught the tip and pulled it up and threw it behind her on the grass.

"You'd better take the bag, too, if you can. The less weight the better." He was already in charge of the situation, thinking more clearly than she was, but his hand, as he lifted the strap over his head, looked dead white and shook uncontrollably. She lowered the crooked end of the stick, and he got the sling over it at the second attempt. Lying full length on the grass and reaching down with the stick, she could just make the distance. She pulled the bag up and threw that, too, behind her. "Right," he said. "Now. See if you can take the strain. It won't be anything like all my weight. It's just that I must have a handhold." She nodded and reached down again with the stick, clinging desperately with both hands to the feruled end. He reached up and caught the crook with one hand, and began to lift himself cautiously out of the water, kicking with his foot for a hold in the soft mud at the bottom of the bank.

For a second or two she stood it, and then her hands began to lose their grip. "No," she said, "no, it's no good, I can't hold on."

It was almost a wail, but he took it calmly enough. "No," he said. "All right. Look, you take the handle and give me the other end." He let go of the stick and let himself down into the water again. "I tell you what," he said. "Can you get a loop of something round the handle? It'll give you more purchase."

She was thinking more clearly herself now, responding to his calmness, and even in a part of her mind determined to be as calm as he was. "All right," she said. "Let me have the stick, and I'll see what I can do. Will you be all right?"

He nodded. He even sketched a smile, but it was not much more than a rictus, and his teeth chattered as he smiled. "I'll be all right," he said, "only be as quick as you can."

She rolled back on the grass and struggled out of her mackintosh. She did not know if it would hold, but it was the best she could do. She tied the sleeves together, taking elaborate care to get a proper knot. Then she turned over onto her front again and wriggled forward to the very edge of the bank. There was no overhang here, and she thought it would be safe enough. She gathered the body of the coat into a roll and took it over her right shoulder from in front and then back under her arm. There was still enough cloth to get a good grip on. Then, very carefully, she hooked the handle of the stick in the loop of tied sleeves and lowered the other end down the bank. It came well within his reach, and he lifted one hand to it. She said, "Wait. Wait, for God's sake, till I'm ready." He started to say something, but contented himself with a nod. She took the bunch of fabric in both hands, working her fingers into the folds and bearing down on it with her full weight as she lay flat on the top of the bank. "All right," she said. "As long as you pull downwards, I think it will be all right. Try not to pull outwards, or you'll have me in on top of you."

"Right," he said. "Take the strain." He had got both hands on the end of the stick now. They were still unsteady, but closed convulsively on it as he began, for the second time, to lift himself clear of the water. The rolled cloth bit into her shoulder and pulled at her clutching hands, but the downward drag anchored her to the grass, so that her shoulder, acting as a sort of human belaying pin, took much of the strain. The full strain was on now, and she thought she could manage it. She watched, hardly daring to breathe, as

Steve began his struggle up the bank. She thought, he's been a climber, he must know what to do.

He was clear of the river now, hanging with one knee against the bank and looking down, while the other foot kicked convulsively at the slippery clay under him. He made a toe-hold to his satisfaction, got the tip of his shoe into it, and began cautiously to straighten the leg. For the moment the strain lightened magically, but she knew that if he lost his foot-hold and fell back, she could not hold him. She said, "Take it slow. For God's sake, take it slow." It was not much more than a whisper. He nodded, breathing noisily, but did not look up. For a moment he stayed there, testing his foot-hold. Then he brought the other leg up and again began kicking at the bank a foot higher up. He was so close, that was the appalling thing. She could have reached out a hand and touched his head, but she had no hand to spare. He secured his second toe-hold, straightened his leg, and then, with a sudden snatch, reached up and got one hand onto the handle of the stick and the knotted cloth it hung in. He took his other hand off the stick, worked the white fingers convulsively for a moment, and then raised that too and laced the fingers of both hands over the handle of the stick. Then he put his face up and smiled at her, this time with more assurance.

"Thank God for that," he said. "I couldn't have held onto that damned stick for much longer. Now we shan't be long." He kicked another toe-hold, and this time when he straightened his leg, his head came level with the bank, so that they stared at each other, almost eye to eye in their desperation, but still there was nothing she could do for him but hold on. "Look," he said, "I'm going to make one more foot-hold, and then try for the top. I must, because I can't get my hands any higher. When I do, grab me by anything you can get hold of, and we'll hope for the best. All right?"

She said, "All right," and he began kicking at his last toe-hold. He took longer about it this time, apparently determined to make it a good one, till she suddenly knew that she could not hold on much longer. "Be quick," she said.

She whispered almost into his ear, and he whispered back. "Right," he said, "now for it." His shoulders rose until they were above the level of her head, but still his hands stayed where they were, grasping the handle of the stick in front of her down-turned face. Then he let go and lunged forward, and at once she let go of the twisted cloth and grabbed at him, so that for a moment or two they struggled with interlocked arms, while he swung one leg up, trying for a grip on the top of the bank. Then, just as she could hold on no longer, he got first a foot and then a knee over the top, and a moment later he had rolled sideways on top of her, a panting mass of waterlogged man, heavy but safe.

He rolled clear of her, and for a moment they both lay there, getting their breath back and loosening their tortured muscles. Then simultaneously, as if at a word of command, they sat up and faced each other. Helen said, "What happened?"

"God knows. I must have got too close to the edge, and the bank gave way under me. One moment I was fishing and the next I was in the water. The stream took me, of course, but it didn't worry me at first. I just went with it under the bank, looking for a place to get out. The trouble was, I couldn't find one, and I began to realise how cold the water was. Then I started to worry a lot. I suppose if you hadn't come, I might have found somewhere, but I don't like the idea much. All I can say is, thank God for you and your stick. Are you all right?"

Helen got to her feet. "I'm all right," she said. "What about you?"

He got up too. "Cold," he said, "bloody cold. Look, if you don't mind, the best thing I can do is to run for home, as fast as I can keep going. That'll warm me, and it will get me out of my wet things quicker. If I do that, can you find your way home?"

"Of course. You do that. I'll bring the stuff."

He looked at her for a moment, uncharacteristically at a loss, as if he did not quite know what to say to her. Then he shivered and pulled himself up. "Right," he said. "I'll be off. You come at your own pace. God willing, you'll find me in a hot bath."

He turned and loped off across the fields, and the grey silence closed round her. She had a momentary urge to go and find the place where he had fallen in, but she did not think it would be easy to find, and she did not want to hang about looking for it. She was afraid now, not specifically afraid for herself, but in dread of the whole dark place. She untied her tortured mackintosh and put it on, and put the bag over one shoulder and the rod over the other. There was no cast or hook, only the reel with a length of loose line hanging from it. The cast must have broken during his struggle in the water. Then she took her stick in her hand and set out on her walk home.

She had gone some way when it occurred to her that he had never asked her what she had been doing there at all. She wondered if he would ask later. She rather thought not. On balance, given the initial error of judgement, she thought he had come well out of the affair, better than she had, but she did not think he would welcome an inquest, all the same. He would make light of it if it was mentioned, and keep it to himself, and presently he would make up his mind to go fishing again or not, as the case might be. But he would not want to discuss it with anyone else. On the whole she was glad. Her mind was still shaken and confused, and presently she would want to talk to someone about it. But she knew it would not be Steve.

Chapter 14

———— ◆ ————

She saw the Fearons' car parked farther along the street as she came into the village. She saw it because she was looking for it. Celia was not in it, and she could not see her anywhere. She slowed and swung her car into the side-street leading to the Fearons' house. She did it impulsively, but it was an impulse rooted in premeditation. She had had a mind to do this if she could, but had not up to then taken a final decision on it. Now she was committed. She felt oddly guilty, avoiding Celia like this, but then her whole relation with her was based on mutual concealment. She left the car outside the gate, so that if Celia came back while she was there, there would be nothing obviously clandestine in her visit. Then she followed the path round to the back of the house. The weather was finer again today, and Charles would be out on his grass plot.

He looked up from his paper as she came round the corner, and his whole face lit up when he saw who it was. "Helen, my dear," he said, "how very nice to see you." He watched her as she came across the grass towards him, and all the time the expression on his face was changing, so that by the time she reached him, he was looking up at her with undisguised concern. She stood there, conscious of little time to spare, but not knowing how to begin, and when he spoke again it was in quite a different voice. "Come on," he said. "Sit down and tell me what's worrying you. No need to lead up to it. I knew there was something, even from the way you walked. So let's have it straight."

She still did not know what she really wanted from him, so she went for the simple fact that had brought her there. "It's Steve," she said. "He went fishing yesterday and fell in the river."

Charles let his breath go in a long sigh. His hands were knotted in his lap, as she had seen them before, and he leant forward in his chair, staring fixedly at her as she sat opposite him. He said, "I presume he got out, at least, and thank God for that. Did he have much trouble?"

She was not going to tell him her part in it, because that would raise questions she did not want to answer, and she thought if she did not mention it, Steve would not. That was if he talked of it at all, which was unlikely. She said, "Yes. I—I think he only just managed it. It wasn't the water, it was the bank. But he said the water was very cold."

Charles nodded. "It would be now," he said. "What exactly happened, do you know?"

Now she could be strictly honest with him again, and felt the relief at once. She said, "He said he was on the edge, and the bank simply gave way under him. It must have been very sudden. He said one moment he was fishing and the next he was in the water."

For a moment Charles was silent. Then he said, "Where was this, do you know?"

"Not exactly. But some way downstream from us. I think there's some place where the fishing looks best."

"You haven't seen the actual place where it happened?"

"No. I don't suppose I could find it, even if I looked. I doubt if he could. The stream took him down, of course."

He nodded. "Was this the first time he's been out?"

"No, the second. The first was some days ago. He caught a couple of small fish, nothing special, but enough to make him want to try again."

He was silent for quite a while then, staring down at his hands. Then he raised his eyes and looked at her very straight. "Why come to me?" he said.

This was it, and still she did not know quite what to say to him. She took the easy way out. "I wanted to talk to someone," she said. "He hasn't talked of it much himself. It may have put him off. I hope it has, obviously. But I don't know. And I don't think it would be any good my saying anything." This was the truth, at least, and something she had not told anyone before. It was up to Charles now.

He spoke suddenly and with unexpected fierceness. He said, "The man's an ass." Then he smiled at her, ruefully and apologetically. "My dear, I'm sorry," he said. "Only some people don't know how lucky they are, and it gets my goat a bit."

She said, "It's all right. Only tell me what you think."

"I think that damned river's dangerous. I've already told you that, and now he's proved it. Did you tell him what I said before?"

She hesitated for a moment and then said, "No."

"I see." He did not ask her why. He understood that now, and she felt enormously relieved that he did understand. He said, "Would it be any good my talking to him?"

"I doubt it. I think half his reason for going to ask Mr. Summers' permission was that you'd rather implied he wouldn't get it."

He gave a sort of small snort and threw his head up, but offered no comment. After a bit he said, "Look, as to the danger, there's nothing more I can tell you. We all know the danger's there. Even he knows it now, whatever he may say or not say. But I tell you one thing: Unless I'm very much mistaken in him, he's not going to put himself in danger again. For all his attitudes, I think he's naturally cautious. He might in fact go fishing again just in order to prove something—to himself, to you, to the world at large—I wouldn't know. But I think that if he does, he'll take damned good care not to get into the water again. And that's all it needs—just taking care. I suppose, not getting too close to the edge and watching where he puts his feet.

Whether he can do that and fish properly I wouldn't know either, but that's up to him. So long as he's careful, he's all right. You must know that. And I think he will be. When were you last by the river?"

"Yesterday morning, in fact."

"By yourself?"

"Yes. I—I wanted to have a good look at it."

"And what did you do when you got there?"

She smiled. She said, "Got down on my hands and knees and crawled to the edge. I felt pretty silly. And when I got there, the bank wasn't dangerous, in fact. I mean, it wasn't undercut or anything. I stood on the edge then. I couldn't have gone in unless someone had pushed me. And of course there was no one there. If there had been, I shouldn't have crawled. I think if there had been anyone there I didn't absolutely trust, I shouldn't have gone near the edge at all. When I say the bank was safe, I only mean that it wouldn't let you down. It wasn't safe in any other way. Once I was down, I couldn't have got up."

He smiled back at her. "Sensible woman," he said. "Well, look, for what it's worth, my own view is that you needn't really worry. I think very likely he may not go out again. He can plead pressure of work or something. But if he does, I don't think he'll put himself in danger." He stopped and looked at her in silence. "I don't know what else I can say," he said. He dropped his eyes to his hands again and sat there, frowning in thought. She knew there was something coming and waited for it. She did not know what it could be. Then he raised his eyes very suddenly and said, "Do you want me to tell Celia about this?"

She thought, matrimonial relations are going cheap today, but she did not know what to say, because she did not know what she wanted. Finally she said, "What do you think?"

He looked at her very straight and spoke with a curious deliberation. He said, "I think she might know more about it than I do."

For a moment they looked at each other in silence. Then she said, "I leave it to you. Tell her if you think it best."

He nodded. "I'll think about it," he said, and Helen got up. There was nothing more to be had from Charles, and she did not want Celia to find her here.

She said, "Thank you, Charles."

He said nothing, but made a sudden, small, helpless gesture with his hands, which moved her more than anything he had said. She left him and went back to the car and drove to the main street of the village. When she got there, she turned left and drove back to Spandles. For all her natural caution as a driver, she did not even look to her right. She did not know whether she wanted to talk to Celia or not. She could talk to Joan, who would be coming tomorrow, because Joan had already warned her of the danger, and she could hardly not tell her that her warning had been justified. But then Joan had nothing more to tell her, or said she had not. If Charles was right, Celia might have. In any case, she knew that it would be up to Celia. Charles might, if he made up his mind to it, tell her about Steve's escape, but he would not suggest that she should speak to her about it. There was too much at stake there. She did not know what Celia would do if he did tell her. There were not many circumstances in which she knew what Celia would do. She could only wait and see.

Meanwhile, Steve seemed none the worse for his adventure, at least physically. If it had shaken him mentally, he was careful not to show it. Outwardly at least he was his usual cheerful self, and was working as usual. The thing had come up only for practical purposes, like drying out his shoes and having his clothes cleaned to get the river mud out of them. Otherwise nothing had been said. She knew why that was. It was because she had seen him for the first time with his defences down and needing her help. She wondered what would happen if he got ill, just as she had wondered what would happen if she did. But neither of them had been ill yet since they were married, and it was no good worrying about that until it happened. Meanwhile the thing lay between them, but it was not the only thing that lay between them now. If he did not refer to it, she certainly would not, and she supposed it would go away in time.

She did tell Joan about it next day as soon as she had picked her up. She would have chosen that moment anyhow, when they were a mile away from Spandles, but in fact it was Joan who gave her the lead. She settled herself next to Helen and said, "Did he go fishing, then?"

Helen said, "He fell in. I had to help him out." She could tell Joan this, as she had been unable to tell Charles.

Joan said, "No! Oh no!" Helen did not turn to look at her, but the distress in her voice was like nothing she had ever sensed in her before. Then Joan asked the question that Helen had not been able to risk Charles' asking. She said, "How did you come to be there?"

"That was your doing. I meant to try and stop him after what you'd said, but when I got back, he'd already gone. I was so frightened, I went after him. I got there just in time. I actually saw him go in, but only from a distance."

Joan said, "There was no one else?"

"No," said Helen, "I had to do what I could by myself." It was only afterwards that she wondered whether this was what Joan had meant.

"What happened then?"

"He said the bank just gave way under him. The stream carried him down a bit. He was holding onto the bank when I got to him, but he couldn't get out, not without help."

"That's it," said Joan. "You can't. That's what they all say. Well, thank God you were there."

Helen said, "Thank you, too. As I said, it was your doing really." They said nothing more all the way.

When they got in, she left Joan to do some cleaning in the kitchen while she went upstairs to do the bed and straighten the room. She went about it slowly, as she did many things now, because she was in no hurry, and had a lot on her mind. It was only as she came downstairs that she heard voices in the kitchen, women's voices. She stood stock-still for a moment, half-way down the stairs. The voices went on, but she could not hear what they were saying. Then she went on down the stairs, opened the kitchen door, and went in.

Celia and Joan stood on opposite sides of the table. They both turned and looked at her as she came in. Both faces were immensely serious. It occurred to her that she had never seen the two of them together before, and she wondered whether they ever met, and what the relation was between them. All she knew was that at the moment, whatever they were thinking, they were both thinking the same thing. They were both, one way and another, guests in her house, but she had the feeling that she was in the presence of a court—not a punitive court, but a court of superior knowledge. The court had to decide what to do about her, and she knew, even as they looked at her, that she had not given them quite long enough to make their decision. She had an immediate instinct to apologise and withdraw, but the ordinary rules of behaviour made this impossible. She had to acknowledge Celia's presence, at least, and it was Celia she looked at. She said, "Hullo, Celia, how nice of you to come."

Celia said, "Hullo, Helen," looking at her and sketching a smile, but her mind, Helen knew, was still with Joan. For what seemed to her a very long time the three women stood there in silence, while the only man in the house went on with his work, also in silence, on the floor above. Helen had a picture of him coming downstairs, perhaps because he too had heard voices in the kitchen, and breaking up with his male inanities what she felt was an immensely important occasion. But it was not nearly time for him to come down yet, and she desperately hoped he would not. She put out a hand and shut the door behind her, as if deliberately shutting him out. It was Joan who finally broke the silence.

She looked at Celia and said, "Well, you'll be wanting to talk to Mrs. Anderson. I'll be getting on upstairs." It was a perfectly correct and normal social speech, but Helen knew that Joan had come to a decision and was telling Celia what she wanted her to do. She saw Joan at that moment as unmistakably the strongest of the three of them, and she noted the fact with a curious, detached satisfaction, because it confirmed an impression she had already formed but not precisely formulated.

Celia, at any rate, accepted it. She said, "Yes, well, I expect you've got things to do," and Joan gathered what she needed together, while the others watched her in silence, and went out, shutting the door behind her. Then Celia turned to Helen, with the necessary hint of a smile on her lips and the familiar deadpan face above it. She said, "Charles told me about Steve's accident, and I wanted to talk to you." She hesitated. Then she said, "Shall we go out, do you think? We can take my car, if you like."

Helen said, "Yes, by all means." She had no alternative, and in any case she wanted to go through with it now, whatever it was. Celia still had her coat on. They went out into the back porch, and Helen put hers on, and they went out of the back door together. Celia's car was standing just inside the gate, because Helen had left hers by the door, for taking Joan back later. They got into the car in silence, and Celia backed and turned it with the expected quiet competence in the limited space available. When they got to the road, she turned right, away from the village.

After a bit she said, "How well do you know Joan Winthrop?"

Helen prevaricated. She said, "Well, I'm getting to know her, of course."

Celia said, "She's a remarkable woman. I can't think why the men can't see it."

Helen said, "Perhaps she won't let them," and Celia said, "I suppose that's it," and they drove on for several minutes in silence. They came to a track leading right-handed down towards the river. It was the same track she and Steve had taken that first day when they had gone down to look at the river. She had not been down it since. It ran between fences, with fields on both sides, but she did not know, here, whose fields they were. She did not suppose in any case it was the river they were looking for. All Celia wanted was a place where they would be unnoticed and undisturbed while they said whatever it was they had to say to each other. In fact, she stopped the car at the place where they had stopped before. The track ended in a small space just big enough to turn a tractor in. It would be a tractor, not a car. She doubted if many cars came this way. She knew the river was quite close in front of her, but she already knew you could not see it from here.

They hardly looked at each other at all, but spoke staring straight in front of them at where the river was. They said the things they had to say, but even now they did not wish to intrude on each other's privacy more than they could help. Celia said, "Charles said Steve was fishing, and the bank gave way under him so suddenly that he was in the water almost before he knew it."

Helen said, "That's right. I was quite close to him. I didn't actually see him go in, because I had stumbled myself. But he was there one moment and gone the next." She assumed as a matter of course that Joan would have told Celia that she had been there.

For a moment Celia hesitated. Then she said, "Are you sure it was an accident?"

Helen let her breath go in a long sigh. "Not altogether," she said, and once more she recognised the truth only when she had spoken it.

Celia said, "Nor am I. It wouldn't be difficult to set a trap like that. You could do it from on top. Cut away the bank from under a section of the edge, and maybe prop it up with sticks or something, I don't know. You didn't see the place afterwards—I mean, the place where he actually went in?"

"No. I—I did have the idea of going and looking for it. That was after Steve had gone off home. But I didn't know if I could find it anyway, and I wanted to get away."

Celia nodded. "I wish you had, all the same," she said.

"But why? Why on earth?" The question was an elliptical one, but Celia knew what she meant.

"Because someone wanted Steve drowned, just as old Wetherby was drowned."

"You don't think that was an accident either? But how can you tell? Charles said you had only just got here, and didn't hear much at the time."

Celia said, "I've learnt more since." Helen said nothing. She did not ask the obvious question, because she found she could not bear to hear it answered. After a bit Celia said, "I think you've got to make up your mind about this. That's what I really wanted to say to you. You've got to make up your mind to warn Steve straight that his life may be in danger, or the thing will go on. Of course, nothing may happen. But you'll never be certain. It's up to you. I know what you're up against, or I think I do. But it's up to you."

For quite a time neither of them said anything. Then Celia said, "Well, that's all I wanted to say. I'll take you home now." She switched on the engine and started to turn the car. Still Helen said nothing, and they drove back to Spandles in silence.

When they got to the end of the drive, Celia said, "I'll drop you here, if I may. I won't come in."

Helen nodded and got out. She said "Thank you" and shut the door, and Celia drove off towards Ladon.

Chapter 15

The next day, Saturday, Helen drove into Skrene after breakfast. She went at least once a week, twice if the list of things that could not be done in Ladon was accumulating too fast. If that did not happen, she went on Saturday, sometimes with Steve, sometimes on her own. Saturday was the big local shopping day, but not market day. The town was busy but not blocked with cattle-trucks, and there was plenty in the shops if you got in early enough. She knew about country shopping. Today Steve had not come with her. She had asked him over breakfast, and he had said, "No, I'm going to work all day today. I'm a bit behind." She noted the "all day" as an assurance that he was not going fishing later. She was not sure if he meant it like that, and if he did, whether it was himself he was assuring or she, but generally he just said "today." He said, "But take your time. I'll get my lunch if you're not back." This too was standard practice, because it was a fair drive each way, and if she had a long list and the shops were crowded, to get back by half past twelve or so meant rushing it, which was tiring and unsatisfactory.

"All right," she said. "I've got quite a lot to do, in fact, but I'll be back as soon as I can." That was not true, because her list was an easy one, but now, as she drove steadily along the quiet country roads, she knew why she had said it. It was because she wanted, if necessary, to have the middle part of the day to herself. She had not at the time made up her mind that it was necessary. Now that it had become possible, she felt the need of it more clearly. She was also conscious of the danger of it, an ill-defined but terrifying danger, but she did not see any other way.

It was all very well for Celia to tell her, presumably with Joan's approval, that she must make up her mind, but they did not realise how little she had to go on. People were always telling her to make up her mind without explaining why, or what they saw as her possible grounds for decision. All right, perhaps Joan had been right, she was indecisive, she was a person who let things happen to her instead of making them happen as she wanted. But she could not act when she could not foresee the consequences of her action. She knew a lot of people did, and she supposed that when things turned out right, they congratulated themselves on having taken a bold decision. But she could not. She had too clear an apprehension of how easily things might turn out wrong. She was paralysed until she knew more, and she knew that there was only one source of knowledge.

She got through her shopping quickly, including taking Steve's things to the cleaners. She wondered, as she handed them in, whether this was one of his reasons, or at any rate one of the reasons he offered himself, for not going fishing. If the woman had asked her, she would have said there was no hurry about them, but the woman merely gave her the ticket and said, "Next Saturday." Even so, it was a week gained, if it would gain a week. She checked over her list, tried, if only to clear her conscience, to think if there was anything more she needed, but could think of nothing. She went back to the car, put her things in the back, and headed out of town. She knew where she was going now. She had not consciously at any point come to a decision, but she knew now what she was doing. When she came to the signpost, she turned right, and now she was no longer heading for Ladon, but north of it. She had been over it all on the map, not because she had made up her mind, but in case she did. She passed some miles north of Ladon and then, after a few miles, turned left-handed until she picked up a signpost pointing left to it. Five miles, it said. She knew where she was now. She was back on the familiar road, the road that ran past Spandles, but she was five miles on the far side of the village.

She had only one more turning to find now, but she knew it would be a small one, and possibly unmarked. It should be about 3½ miles ahead. She had measured it on the map. She checked the reading on the milometer and settled down to drive 3 miles and then slow down and watch for the turning. There was no mistaking it, in fact, when she came to it, even without the milometer reading. It was very narrow, but tarmac had been laid, with a strip of grass on each side. It would rate a thin double line on the map. It was sign-posted to some place or other she did not know, but this did not worry her. She was not going far along it. She turned into it, going very slowly now, and after a few hundred yards found what she was looking for, a field-gate with a comfortably wide opening. She did not try to get her car in through the gate, but parked it so that she did not block either the gateway or the lane. She was country-woman enough for that. Then she got out, locked the car, and walked to the gate. The light was grey and the air still, and after the noise of the car the silence was absolute.

The gate was tied up with wire, and she would have to climb over it anyhow, but when she had both feet on the second bar up, and was ready to swing a leg over, she stopped, holding the top rail with both hands, and looked eastwards across the fields. She saw Calton at once. There were no buildings between her and it, and for all she knew she might already be on Calton land, or would be when she had climbed the gate. From here it was much more clearly an island site than it was when seen from the east, because the land fell away from it more sharply on this side. Of course, in this flat landscape the differences in height were small, but the group of buildings, brick and timber, with the brick farmhouse in the middle, stood up on its green mound like a city of the plain. When the water was over the fields, you would see its image reflected below it, or at night its lights shining double, like a ship at sea. Away to the left, across the dip in the ground, she could see the huddled roofs and church tower of Ladon. It was impossible to tell from here, with the long dip in between, that they stood higher than Calton, but she knew they did. She swung herself over the gate and set out across the fields.

For several minutes she walked with an almost grim determination, and then suddenly, high up on her right hand, the clouds parted, and in a moment the level fields were flooded with pale sunshine, as they had been that first day when they had gone to see Spandles. Illogically but undeniably, she was aware of a sudden lifting of the spirit, and even of a flicker of anticipatory excitement. Whatever she had been to start with, she was on Calton land now. Every fence between her and the buildings was at some point gated, and they did not put gates in boundary-fences. Matthew Summers had said that if she came onto his ground, she must expect to meet him, and now she was on his ground, and still hurrying on. Like fair Janet, she thought, away to Carterhaugh as fast as she could hie, looking for Tam Lin. Good sense rejected the comparison, but Helen smiled as she rejected it. Her sense of danger had gone completely. The brick buildings stood up rose-red and silent in the yellow light, and there was a brooding peace over the whole wide landscape, as there had been, once, in the lamp-lit rooms inside. She went from gate to gate, and opened them, and went through, shutting them carefully behind her. It was only the gate on the lane that had been wired, and she had climbed that. She went through the last gate, and now for the first time felt the ground rising steadily under her. She climbed the green slope towards the silent buildings, knowing with an absolute certainty that he was somewhere among them, only she did not know where.

She skirted a Dutch barn stacked to the roof with golden hay-bales and found herself in a paved yard. Even the paving was brick here. The house was in front of her—the back of the house, she supposed—and there were buildings all round her. She was half-way across the yard when suddenly, in the corner of her eye, she saw movement on her right, and when she turned, he was standing in a doorway, half in the sunlight and half in shade, looking at her and smiling. He said, "By God, I'm glad to see you." He spoke very quietly in his slow, deep voice, but she heard him clearly in the silence. He did not move. For a moment she stood and looked at him, and then she turned and went over to him. She went all the way across the yard to him, head back, hands hanging at her sides, and still he had not moved.

Even when she got to him, he did not ask her why she had come, or how it was she came from the west and not the east. It was as if he already knew that, and she was prepared to believe he did, even if his explanations were different from those she had been offering herself. Or perhaps it was simply that to him none of this mattered, and she was not sure now that it mattered to her. What mattered was that she was here, and he was glad to see her. He said, "I was just seeing to Buttercup. You know her."

She could see the silky, dappled flanks in the shadow behind him. If he was right, this was actually the creature she had once, for a minute or two, had close and agonising mental relations with, but now it looked to her like any other cow. It was the name her mind fastened on, because it was ridiculous that there really should be a cow called Buttercup. It was like being introduced to a farmer called Giles or a smocked farm-labourer called Hodge. She giggled and said, "Buttercup?" and his brows came together suddenly.

"Certainly," he said. "We've always had a Buttercup at Calton. It's a very good name for a cow."

He said it perfectly seriously, with a touch of patient exasperation, as if he were explaining things to a rather silly child. Half the time, she thought, he spoke to her as if she was a child, but she knew he thought of her as a woman, and this was unfair of him, because it made him extraordinarily difficult to deal with. He had turned to the cow again, though she could not see what he was doing to it, and she spoke apologetically to his back. "Of course," she said. "It was only—" Her explanation died away, because she saw, when she came to look at it, that her explanation was much sillier than the cow's name. For a moment she stood there, stricken with her own silliness, but then he gave the cow a final pat and turned to her again, and her misgivings melted in the warmth of his smile. There was so much warmth in him, that was what disarmed her. It underlay all his habitual solemnity, and when it broke through, it was as shattering in its effect as the sunlight suddenly flooding that sombre landscape. Charles Fearon had warmth, too, but it was a gentle, inward warmth. This had the radiant energy of a fire in a cold room, so that she instinctively held out her hands to it.

"Oh," he said, "never mind Buttercup." He took her gently by the upper arm, and turned her and walked across the yard with her, and she went with him as placidly as a child goes with a sympathetic grown-up who has taken it by the hand. "There's no one else here," he said, "not at this time on a Saturday. There'll be a man in presently for the milking, but you'll not have long in any case." He said it to re-assure her, and she realised suddenly how worse than useless all her precautions would have been if there had been a man here from the village to see her come and go. She had not given that a thought, but she was grateful for the assurance now it was offered. She still had things to say to him, only she could not say them now.

They walked round the end of the house and came into the yard that Buttercup had brought her into that first night. Then they had come, she and the cow, as fugitives from the river and the threatening darkness, but now there was nothing anywhere but this serene sunlight on the empty fields. They came to the door, and there he stopped for a moment and stood looking eastwards, head back, eyes half-closed, like an animal testing the wind for danger.

She knew, immediately and instinctively, what the danger was he had in mind. She said, "You're thinking of the river."

He turned and looked down at her. The movement was as slow as all his movements, but his concentration was absolute, and she thought that another man, taken off his guard like that, would have whipped round to face the challenge. His eyes had widened in the way they did, and there was no smile on his face now. Then he nodded twice, and let his breath go in what was almost a sigh. He said, "We're always thinking of the river at Calton. We've always had to. We're at its mercy, especially now." She supposed he meant at this season of the year, but did not feel altogether sure. He said, "I wondered if you knew that."

She nodded, looking up into his dark eyes, but did not say anything.

"It could drown Calton," he said. "It did once, generations back. It wouldn't have the buildings down, but it could ruin everything and drown half the stock. It could drown a man, too, if it could wash him off the high ground. It's a terrible river."

She said, "I know. It frightens me. It always has, ever since we came."

He gave that strange double nod, still looking down at her. "You understand," he said. "There is a great deal you could understand. You're not like the rest. You're an innocent. Never be ashamed of your innocence, even if it puts you at the mercy of the others. You're the most beautiful creature I've ever seen or dreamed of, but it's your innocence that makes you so special, for all that. I could love you if I let myself, do you know that? I've never thought to love anybody. I wouldn't dare. But I could love you, only what's the use?" He shook himself suddenly, as if out of pa-

tience with his own despair. "But try not to be afraid of the
river," he said. "I told you, it won't drown you. Never make
light of it, but don't be afraid of it." For a moment she
fought to find words for what she had to say, but he took
her arm suddenly and opened the door and drew her inside,
and then the moment was gone.

When they came out of the house, the whole look of the
world had changed. The sunlight was gone from the fields,
and a heavy pall of cloud covered the whole sky, darkening
steadily to the eastern horizon, which faced them as they
came out of the door. Here under the lee of the house the air
was as still as ever, but overhead the cloud-bank moved
slowly eastwards, and she knew that when she came to walk
back to the car, she would walk into the westerly breeze,
light but persistent and chilly, which always brought this
kind of weather to Ladon. Matthew Summers stopped at
once and stood for a moment as he had stood earlier, looking eastwards across the fields. But now his head was down
and he looked, not like an animal questing, but like a man
calculating, a man who observed and did not like what he
saw. She did not break in on his thoughts now, nor did he
share them with her. He said, "I'd best be getting the beasts
in," but he said it to himself, and so quietly that she could
only just catch the words. He was face to face with his he-
reditary enemy, and she left them to their confrontation.

Then he turned and took her by the arm again, and they
went northwards along the front of the house. They never,
she thought, held hands as lovers might. There was not that
sort of mutuality in the relation between them. Instead he
took her arm, gently but so that she could always feel the
elastic strength in his arm, and held her to him, guiding her
steps alongside his. When they turned the corner of the
house, the breeze met them, as she had known it would, and
she knew that, unless she walked briskly, she would be cold
before she got to the car. They went across the yard and
round the Dutch barn, still in silence, and started on the

long green slope down towards the first gate. When they got there, he opened the gate to let her through, but did not go through it with her. Instead, he swung it shut and fastened it, and she turned, and they faced each other over the bars of the gate.

For a moment he looked down at her, with his eyes, dark and suddenly opaque, boring down into hers. Then he said, "You'd best tell me what it was you came to say."

She nodded, conscious for the first time of her earlier fear, and could find only the basic words for what was in her mind. "It's Steve," she said, "my husband. He fell in the river. He was fishing."

He did not move a muscle. "But he got out?" he said.

She nodded again, looking up at him dry-mouthed. "I helped him out," she said. "I don't think he could have done it otherwise."

He let his breath go, and this time there was no mistaking the sigh. She had heard it before. He said, "You? You of all people," and that too she had heard him say before.

She did not say anything, because there was nothing she could say, but his face was suddenly gentle again. He said, "You'd best be going now," and she turned without a word and went off into the chilly breeze, back to where she had left the car. She walked steadily and did not once look back.

Chapter 16

It had been raining all night, lightly but persistently. She knew, because she had hardly slept at all. You could not hear the rain itself, but you could hear things dripping that only dripped when it was raining. It was so dark when she got out of bed that she checked the clock on the bedside table with her watch on the dressing-table, to make sure it really was the time it said, and when she went to the window, she could only just see that it was still raining. There was nothing else to see except the horizon, where the grey of the sky met the total darkness of the land. There was no detail anywhere. She shivered and put on her dressing-gown and opened the door very quietly. She went straight down to the kitchen. There was nothing to dress for today, however late Steve slept, and she wanted her tea very badly. When she put on the bright kitchen lights, it might still have been night outside the windows. She wondered whether, if she had looked for them, she could have seen the lights of Calton. You could see them at night out of the western window, but it was the southern window she had looked out of, and she was not going to risk going up again to look for them now.

When she had made the tea, she pulled out a chair and sat at the table with the tea-things in front of her. Generally she drank her early-morning tea standing up, moving about between sips to do things in the kitchen, but today she felt nervously and mentally exhausted, and wanted only to sit. The clock ticked steadily, but she did not like the sound of it. There was too much time now, and she did not know what to do with it. It was Sunday today, and Joan would not be coming, and Steve would be working all day, pressed as he was. She thought later, perhaps after breakfast, she would try to sleep, but only in her chair in the sitting-room when Steve was once more upstairs. She did not feel sleepy now, only desperately in need of sleep. It was no good trying to think. She had been at that all night, and no good had come of it. She left her mind a blank and concentrated on the tea, because that was the only thing she could see any good in.

By the time she had finished it, she could see that it was lighter outside, and when she turned the kitchen lights off, she found grey daylight everywhere, and saw that it had stopped raining. She was conscious of an immediate relief, but knew there was no good reason for it. It had not been raining hard enough to do any harm, and in any case it was not the rain falling here that mattered. All the same, there was relief in it, because at least it made it easier for her to get out of the house, and she knew she would need that later, not because she would be wanting to go anywhere in particular, but simply because she would want to get away. The fields would not be too wet for walking if you wore boots. She could have gone and seen Charles, only today he would be indoors and Celia would be at home, and with Charles tied as he was, there was always the chance that she might at some point find herself alone with her, and she did not want that. She thought very probably Celia would not want it either, but she could not be sure. She even wondered what Joan would be doing in her spotless bungalow on a grey Sunday, but she supposed that Jack would be at home. Knowing him, she felt sure he would work on a Sunday if there was work that needed doing, or with Ernie off he might be keeping an eye on the pumps. But he could do that without leaving the house, and he was a man who would read a Sunday paper, almost certainly the *Observer*, looking for something to be indignant about. For a moment, with an unexpected touch of wry amusement, she contemplated the three disparate marriages, and thought that she and Charles and Joan, even today, could manage to be cheerful over coffee, but the other three together did not bear thinking about.

She pushed her chair back with unnecessary violence and got up. It was no good going on like this. The best cure for nervous exhaustion was physical activity, and there were still things to be done, even on a grey Sunday and with Steve still asleep upstairs. He would be awake presently and wanting his tea and then his breakfast, and she did not want him to find her in this state of mental and physical disarray. She got rid of her own tea-things and set out his on a tray, so that she could take it straight up to him if he did not come down and make it for himself. Then she went upstairs and opened the bedroom door and put her head in. He was still asleep. She gathered up her things, tip-toeing about the room in her slippers with one eye always on the bed. Then she went out as quietly as she had come in and made for the bathroom. She was hardly dressed and down in the kitchen again when she heard him coming downstairs after her, whistling tunelessly but cheerfully.

She was glad he was cheerful, because when he was, he always assumed that other people were too, and that made it much easier for her to conceal her own wretchedness. It was a very private wretchedness, and if she had to account for it, her explanation would have to be false. So long as she did not have to lie to him, she at least would not feel guilty. There had been a time when she could have made a virtue of hiding her own unhappiness in the face of his happiness, but she was past that stage now. She tried to avoid deceiving him more than was absolutely necessary, but she no longer even tried to deceive herself.

As soon as he came in, his face confirmed the cheerfulness of his whistle. He said, "Hullo, you're up and dressed. Sorry

I'm late. I worked a bit late. But it's going better now. I reckon I'm on time again."

"That's good," she said. She had put the kettle on as soon as she heard him coming downstairs. She said, "Would you like to take your tea upstairs while I get on with the breakfast?" It was on the face of it a perfectly kindly suggestion, but she knew she very badly wanted him to accept it. She could not do with him and his cheerfulness this morning more than she had to.

He said, "Yes, all right. I shan't be long." He wandered to the window and looked up at the sky while she made the tea. There was not much to look at from here except the strip of northern sky over the out-buildings. He said, "It's going to clear later, I think, but everything looks pretty wet now. It must have rained a bit during the night."

"Very likely," she said. She put the teapot on the tray, and he picked it up and took it off upstairs. He did not try to shut the door with the tray in his hands, and when he was half-way up the stairs, she went over and shut it. For a moment she stayed there, leaning back with her weight against the shut door, as if to shut out something that was trying to get in. But there was nothing there, or if there was, the door was no use against it. She took herself away from it and set about getting breakfast.

He was still cheerful when he came down, but a little out of touch, as if he had something on his mind that he had laid aside only to come and have breakfast, and would get back to as soon as he went upstairs again. The meal went quickly and mostly in silence, though the silence was a perfectly amiable one. She supposed it must be something to do with the book. Whatever it was, she welcomed it, just as she had welcomed his cheerfulness. She had really very little against him at all except his mere presence, almost, she thought, his mere existence, and that was not his fault. She was not conscious even of any intense emotional strain in herself, of pent-up feelings that would erupt as soon as he was gone. The only strain she experienced was in a curious way the counterpart of her feelings for him, the strain of pretending to be there when she was hardly there at all. She felt like an actor in a bad play, doing everything carefully in character, but never for a moment convincing herself of the character's existence.

When he had gone back upstairs, she did what she had to do and went to the back door and looked out. The sky was still overcast, but the cloud was higher and thinner, and did not move at all. The air was utterly still and not particularly cold, but reeking with moisture, so that she felt its chill in her nostrils as she breathed. She put on mackintosh, head-scarf, and boots, and went out, shutting the door quietly behind her. She wanted to go down to the fields, but did not want him to see her go, because that would destroy her privacy. She did not know whether he looked out of his window at all during his working sessions, but it was a risk she could not take. She went half-way along the drive leading to the road, and then turned and climbed over the left-hand fence and set off south-westwards, at an angle that would bring her out onto the fields some way west of the house. The side of the spur on which the house stood sloped very gradually here, but after a bit she was level with the fields on her left, and then she turned full west and went on, walking parallel with road and river, but this time much nearer the road.

She walked merely for the sake of walking. She was not going anywhere, simply occupying time and trusting to the exercise to loosen her over-taut mind and bring on the sleepiness she still did not feel. Measured time meant very little to her. There was nothing she need get back to except lunch. She would walk as long as she felt like walking, and then turn and walk back. She did not know, in fact, how long it was before she decided to turn, but at last she did turn and face back towards the east again, and when she did, she stopped and caught her breath, suddenly horrified

at what she saw. The whole sky eastwards was a hanging
curtain of purple cloud, so dense that it seemed to foreclose
on the horizon itself, completely blotting out the distant
hills. There was no motion or turbulence in it, simply a long
dark bank that lay upon the country, and could not move
because there was no wind to move it. For a moment or two
she stared at it, and then she set off again, hurrying home
now, although even when she got there there was nothing
she could do but wait.

She took off her walking things in the porch and ran upstairs on stockinged feet. Steve's door was shut, but the bedroom door was open, and she was into it without a sound
and almost flattening her nose against the glass of the southern window. But there was nothing to see. The empty
fields fell gently away in front of her in the grey light, and
beyond them the flat country rose again, and somewhere in
between, the river still ran invisibly in its deep-cut channel.
For all she knew it might stay there. For all she knew that
dreadful curtain of hanging cloud might not empty itself
onto the hills the river came from, but she did not really believe it, and when she went to the western window, there
was not a beast to be seen anywhere on the fields. Away at
almost invisible Calton Matthew Summers was watching the
eastern sky too, and he did not trust it any more than she
did. Behind his shut door Steve worked silent and uncon-
cerned, but on her an oppression lay like lead.

Lunch was a repetition of breakfast but mercifully even
shorter, and when she had cleared it and he had gone upstairs again, she wandered through into the sitting-room, and
shut the door behind her, and settled herself in her chair.
She longed for sleep if only to escape from her misery, but
did not know if it would come to her. She shut her eyes and
lay back, wooing it as unhappy people have always wooed
it, with longing but with no great hope. She did not know,
afterwards, how long she had waited for it, because afterwards her mind was too full of other things to be interested.

She woke with a stiff neck and a grinding headache, and when she looked at her watch, she saw with dismay that it was past four. Already the room was almost dark. She heaved herself out of her chair and went blindly through into the kitchen, looking for the aspirin she kept in the kitchen cupboard. It was only when she went to fill a glass with water that she saw the cup in the sink. Steve must have come down and found her asleep and made himself some tea without waking her. She took her aspirin, but already the headache had eased with the mere easing of her cramped neck. She made a pot of tea and filled two cups. She drank one at once, as hot as she could get it down. The other she took upstairs as a sort of sin-offering for her negligence. She opened the door of Steve's room quietly and took the cup in, but there was no one there. She put the cup down and went out onto the landing again. An unreasoning panic seized her, and she called "Steve! Steve! Where are you?" but no one answered. She called again, almost screaming now in the dark, silent house, but wherever he was, he was not there. She ran down to the back door and looked out, and saw both cars in the garage. She shut the door and ran upstairs again, but this time she ran to the south-facing window on the landing and looked out. The picture was darker, but had not changed. She still could not see the river.

It was only then that she wondered for the first time whether he had, after all, gone fishing. She remembered his cheerfulness and preoccupation, as if he had something in mind he did not want to tell her. She remembered his saying he was no longer pressed for time. The picture fitted. The only thing against it was that his usual fishing clothes were still at the cleaners, but there was not much in that. It might have served him as an excuse if he had not wanted to go fishing, but would not stop him if he did. Within reason, she supposed you could fish in anything. Obviously his fishing-tackle was the thing, but she did not know enough about it to be certain. He had several rods, which he kept hanging in cloth cases on one wall of his room, but she did not know how many there ought to be. She went into his room again, looking for evidence that he had changed his clothes and taken some of his tackle, but could find nothing conclusive. The room was untidy anyway when you considered it in detail, and his working clothes were so casual that he might have gone out on an impulse without changing anything at all. She wondered whether he had had the impulse only when he had found her asleep. He must have known she would try to persuade him not to, and she saw him taking advantage of her sleep to slip out and go fishing, just as he had taken advantage of her absence before to slip out and ask Matthew Summers' permission to fish. It went with the small-scale deviousness in Steve that she had grown accustomed to. But again she remembered his frame of mind earlier in the day. He might well have already decided to go out if he could, even perhaps in some way overcome his own admitted fear of it and talked himself into the venture. All she knew for certain was that he had left the house while she was asleep and had not taken his car. And she knew he was a man who, unlike her, never walked for pleasure.

In any case, there was nothing she could do now. It was much too late to go after him, and already too dark to see him at any distance. For all she knew, he might have gone upstream instead of down. But he would have to be back soon. She had an idea fishermen preferred a grey light, but surely no one could fish in near-darkness. There was nothing for it but to wait, and in the meantime to tell herself, as Charles had told her, that if he was fishing, he would be fishing very circumspectly. That too was in character. It would be the fact that he had, despite his previous misadventure, gone out that would be important to him, not whether he caught anything when he was out.

She went round the house putting lights on. She even left a light burning on the upstairs landing and the curtains undrawn, so that he would have a light to steer by if he really got himself benighted. Then she went into the kitchen and set herself, with an almost mechanical concentration, to get their supper. The clock ticked maddeningly, but she would not let herself look at it. Time was running away with her now, and she could not bear the sound of it, let alone the sight.

She finished what she had to do in the kitchen and went through into the dining-room to lay the table. She laid it with elaborate care, but at last could find nothing more to do, and went back into the kitchen again. Desperation was welling up in her now, but still there was nothing she could do. She sat down at the table and put her elbows on it and her head on her hands. She tried to think clearly what she would have to do if he did not come back, but did not know where she would start. She would give him another quarter of an hour, and then do something. She raised her eyes for the first time to look at the clock, and as she did so she heard the back door open.

She pushed her chair back and got to her feet, but now her whole instinct had gone into reverse. The one thing she must not do was rush out and question him. She must let him get his things off and come in in his own time.

But he did not wait to get his things off. He came straight to the kitchen door and pushed it open and walked in. His face was white and drawn. He had his fishing-bag still slung on his shoulder, but nothing in his hand. He pulled out a chair and slumped down on it, and it was only then she saw that he was wet from head to foot.

She said, "Oh God, Steve, you've fallen in the river again."

He lifted his head and looked at her as she stood over him. His eyes were bewildered, as if he could not quite believe what he had to say. He said, "I didn't fall. I was pushed. Summers pushed me."

Chapter 17

Like him, though for different reasons, she could hardly bring herself to believe what he said, and yet knew it to be true. She did not, as she ought to have done, say "Matthew Summers?" She could not say the name at all. She said instead, "Steve, what do you mean? What happened?"

He put his face down, almost as if looking up at her in the bright light hurt his eyes. He sat hunched in his chair and spoke to the kitchen table, and when he spoke, his voice had anger in it, a snarling anger she had never heard before. He said, "Well, just that. I was fishing. I was standing a safe distance from the edge of the bank. I didn't want to make a fool of myself a second time. It was starting to get dark, and I knew I'd have to pack it in soon. He must have come up behind me. At any rate, I didn't see him until he was right up to me. I was watching the water, of course. I didn't even hear anything until the last second. Then I heard a movement behind me and swung round, as one does. I was only half round when he hit me, but it was him, all right. He hit me with his whole weight in the small of my back and almost lifted me off my feet. I hadn't a hope, of course. I just went straight over the edge into the water."

She said, "But—but couldn't it have been an accident?" She almost pleaded with him, but he still did not look up.

"Accident my foot," he said. "It was murder—attempted murder, anyway. I mean, he didn't try to pull me out, did he? I never saw him again. I expect he had a look for me in the water, but I never saw him. Well, I didn't try."

She said nothing for a moment. Then she said, "What did you do?"

"Went with the stream, the same as I did before, but it's running a lot faster now. I got as close under the bank as I could. It was the one idea I had, to get away from him. I knew he'd never go away as long as he thought I was still afloat. I went downstream as fast as I could until I found an overhanging stretch of bank. It was pretty dark by then. I got right in under it and hung on with only my head and my hands out of the water and waited for him to go. I knew it was my only hope. I thought if he couldn't see me anywhere, he'd reckon I'd gone under, and that would satisfy him. I waited as long as I dared, but the water was hellish cold, and I couldn't leave it too long. After a bit I went down to a better bit of bank and climbed out."

"But how?" she said. "How did you get out? You couldn't before."

Then at last he raised his face and looked at her, and grinned suddenly. It was a grin of almost malicious triumph. He heaved the bag off his shoulder and put it down on the floor beside him. For a moment he leant down and foraged about in it, and then he took something out and threw it on the table with a metallic clang. It was a long steel spike with a broad ring at the blunt end. She had never seen anything like it before. "Pitons," he said. "A relic of my climbing days. I thought of them yesterday, and dug them out of one of my boxes. They're meant for rock, of course. You have to hammer them in. But I reckoned you could drive them into the bank by hand, and they'd hold. Well, they did, in fact. I took four of them in my bag when I went out. They were a bit of a drag, but it was worth it." He looked at her again, this time with a sort of defiance. He said, "I don't think I'd have had the nerve to go out again without them. I was bloody scared that last time. And I badly wanted to go out. I wanted to make myself, like making yourself drive again after a crash. I felt better, just knowing I had them. And I was right, you see? They worked, in fact. I got up without too much difficulty, and put my head up over the top and looked for him. That was the worst part, because I knew if he saw me, I shouldn't have a second chance. But I couldn't see him anywhere. I got out and ran like hell for home. I had to leave the other pitons in the bank, of course. I lost my best rod, too, damn him."

There was nothing for her now but total surrender. She was at the mercy of events again. She said, "What are you going to do?"

"Do?" he said. "Go to the police, of course. The man's a raving lunatic. I expect he did the same to old Wetherby. But there's no great hurry, as I see it. He'll assume I'm drowned, and be lying low. I'm going to get myself warm and dry, and then go to the police. In Skrene, I suppose. I reckon they'll find Mr. Summers safe at Calton when they go for him. So long as he doesn't know I got away."

He stood up with such sudden violence that the chair tipped over and clattered on the floor behind him. He did not pick it up. He did not look at her at all, but just went to the door. He had left it open when he came in, and it was still open. He went straight out through it and along the hall, and a moment later she heard him going up the stairs. For the second time that day she shut the door and leant back against it, looking at the brightly lit kitchen. She looked at the supper things ready by the stove, and the fallen chair, and the sodden bag on the floor, and that single bright steel pin lying on the table. She had got over the shock now, and was suddenly afraid. For the first time since she had met him, she was afraid of Steve. She had felt guilty before, but never frightened, and now she was. It was the unexpected violence in him, and the way he had avoided her eye, except to grin at her when he produced the piton.

Then she told herself that that was nonsense. He might feel her lack of sympathy. He probably did. He was sensitive to things like that. But he had no possible reason to suspect anything between her and Matthew Summers, and he had coupled the attack on him with the death of old Wetherby. A raving lunatic, he had called him. She revolted at that, knowing, with a sudden dreadful clarity, who was, for her, still the better man of the two. Anger, unexpected but welcome, came to her aid. She took herself away from the door and picked up the fallen chair and put it in its place by the table. She picked up the bag, still oozing water onto the kitchen floor, and dropped it in the sink. Only the piton she left where it was on the table. She did not like the look of it and did not want to touch it. She got a cloth and mopped up the floor, and dropped the cloth, too, in the sink. She did all this with a calm deliberation. Then there was nothing to do until he came downstairs again, and she stood there, doing nothing, waiting for him to come.

He did not take long. He did not even go along to the bathroom. She would have heard him if he had. For all his saying there was no hurry, he was eager to be off after his revenge. She heard him coming downstairs again, and knew that he would have left his wet clothes lying on the floor of his room for her to pick up after he had gone. He did not even come into the kitchen. He just opened the door and looked in at her. He still looked pale, but he was very spruce and trim, as if he had been at pains to make himself a convincing witness. For a moment they looked at each other through the open door. Then he said, "I'm off now. Don't know how long I'll be. Better not wait supper for me."

She nodded and said, "All right," and he turned and went out of the back door, and presently she heard his car start and through the window saw its lights swing in the yard as he ran it out and turned it. Then it accelerated and was gone, and silence settled once more over the house.

She did not hesitate at all. She did not even go upstairs to pick up his wet things. She was in a hurry now herself. She went out into the porch and put on her mackintosh and boots, and tied her headscarf over her head. She would have liked to take her car, but dared not risk it. In any case, there was time. Skrene was some way away, and she supposed there would be formalities of a sort when he got there. She took her stick and a torch and went out, shutting the door behind her. She was not sure, as she did so, whether she would ever come back into it again. She hurried along the garden and down the steps, and set off across the fields towards Calton.

She had expected pitch darkness, but found to her surprise that there was a watery moon. It was still in its first quarter, and westering already, but the sky had cleared enough to let it through. There was nothing you could call moonlight, no visible light and shade. It was just not perfectly dark, and the slim, hazy slip of moon hung in the sky, almost ahead of her now as she walked. She hurried, but used her stick consciously and did nothing rash. She was obsessed with the need to get there. She did not examine the reasons behind her need, though she knew it was not only the police she was thinking of. All she knew was that Matthew Summers believed Steve dead, drowned in the river, and that he had to be told as soon as possible that he was not.

She saw the lights of Calton long before she got there. There were not many of them, and she could not tell from here where they were, but she could see them, and knew he was there. She assumed he would be alone, and at this time of a Sunday evening the assumption was a fair one, but she would not have hesitated even if she had known he was not. Things had got far beyond concealment now. When she came at last into the yard, she saw the lights were in the out-buildings to her left, and she ran towards them, surefooted now on the flat paving of the yard, calling as she ran. She thought she seemed to spend a lot of her time now calling to invisible men, but it was only an incidental oddity in the sudden total disintegration of her life. She called, "Matthew Summers! Matthew Summers!" She had never called him anything before, not speaking to him directly, and the full name came naturally to her. She still had not reached the nearest lighted doorway when she saw his tall figure against the lights. He came to her across the yard and took her by the shoulders and held her there, not quite against him but not at arm's length, looking down at her up-tilted face in the wan light of the moon and the glimmer of yellow light from the open door. He did not say anything. He just waited for her to tell him what she had come to say.

She knew, this time, what she had to say. She said, "My husband isn't dead. He got out of the river. He's gone to the police."

She could not see his face very clearly, because what light there was was all behind him, but she felt, even through his arms as they held her, the deep shattering sigh that shook his whole body. "Not dead?" he said. "Not dead?" There was no anger or consternation in his voice, only an overwhelming despair.

She shook her head at him. "He's gone to the police," she said again. "They'll be here soon."

He shook his head back at her, a slow double shake like his strange double nod. "They won't," he said. "The river will. You don't understand. The river will come tonight. It had to have its life and hasn't had it. You must try to understand. I tried to give it Buttercup, but you brought her back. Then I tried to give it your husband, even though I thought him the lesser beast, and you got him back too. You of all people. And now I've tried one last time to give him to the river, and again he's come back. And it's seven years gone, more than seven now, and the river's not been paid. It will be here, all right."

She could not reason with him, not because the thing was beyond reason, but because she believed what he said. She said, "I didn't know. I didn't know. How could I know?" begging his pardon for having saved her husband's life, and again he shook his head at her.

"No," he said, "no, you couldn't know. But that's finished now. It's all finished. I can't give you to the river. I told you." He spoke of it as a reasonable course of action that for reasons of his own he found impossible. She felt no fear of him at all. "In any case," he said, "what's the use now?" He took his eyes from hers and looked eastwards, as she had seen him look before. Then he said, "You must go or it will be too late. You mustn't stay here. You must go now."

She pushed his arms aside and clung to him, almost shaking him in her desperation. "But you can go too," she said. "We can both go, can't we? There's still time. You can't send me back by myself. Where am I to go now?"

He was suddenly perfectly calm again. "You can go and make a life for yourself," he said. "Of course you can, and you so beautiful." He was talking to her as if she were a child again, almost wheedling her. "It's time you got on your own feet, anyhow, and made your own life instead of having everything decided for you. Especially by him. He's no good to you, that one, or ever will be. And he'll find someone else easily enough. You don't have to worry about him. So you go and do that. That's all you can do for me now, do you see? Promise me you'll do that. It's different for me. You can see that, if you'll just think. There's no life for me except at Calton, and they aren't going to leave me here now, are they? But at least the place and the beasts needn't suffer for it. Nor the village either. That's my responsibility, and always has been, from generations back. So I'll see to that. I'll go and talk to the river. We can strike a bargain, I don't doubt, even as late as this. But you must be gone before the river comes."

He lifted his head and looked eastwards again, and suddenly she felt him stiffen. But he still kept his voice calm. He said, "Look now, if you don't believe me."

She turned and looked where he pointed, and saw the flat whiteness spread over the dark fields under the faint light of the moon. Fear seized her suddenly, a moment of blind panic like the senseless panic of the tethered cow, but he took her by the arm and walked her calmly across the yard towards the gate, and she went with him unresisting. "All right?" he said. "Come on, then, we'd best hurry, or the water will be over the road."

They walked briskly on, through the two open gates and down the slope towards the village. Then he caught his breath suddenly and said, "Run," and they ran side by side, with his hand still holding her arm. A moment later there was water round their feet. He stopped. He said, "Go on. You must go on. It won't be deep yet, up to your knees maybe, but no worse. But you must keep going. You know what you've got to do. Just you go and do it. Promise?"

She said, "I promise," and he pushed her away from him, and she could not even turn back to look at him. She went on, because that was what he had told her, and there was nothing else she could do. There was a broad stretch of water ahead of her, moving across from right to left, but she could see the line of the road on the far side and knew where she had to go. She splashed on through the water, and it got deeper until it filled her boots, and still she kept on walking steadily through it. She would have been glad of her stick now, but must have dropped it in the yard. Now the water was up to her knees, and over her knees, and she went through it laboriously, panting with the effort, but concentrating mindlessly on the mere business of survival. Then at last the road rose under her feet, and she was walking uphill again. For a little the rise of the water kept pace with the rise of the road, but at last it started to fall away from her legs and she could move more freely.

It was as she came out of the last of the water that the lights flared suddenly in front of her, blinding her. She stopped there on the edge of the water, shielding her eyes with her hand, as the car came down the road towards her. It was coming fast, but at once she heard the tyres screaming on the road as it braked. The driver had seen her now, and he had also seen the water. The car came to a halt not three yards from her. A door swung open and a man got out. He did not bother with her at all at first. He just walked past her and stared at the stretch of water ahead. He was a policeman in uniform. She could see the peaked cap as he turned. Then he came up to her and said, "What are you doing here?"

"I'm going home," she said.

"Are you?" he said. "Where from, then?"

She was suddenly icy in her defiance. "Calton," she said. "Where else would I be coming from?"

He nodded. "That's right," he said. "Have you seen Mr. Summers?"

"Oh yes," she said. "He's there, at Calton."

"Is he, now? Well, that's all right, then. I'll want to talk to you later perhaps, but I won't trouble you now. If you'd just give me your name?"

"Anderson," she said. "Mrs. Anderson. I live at Spandles."

His head went up with a jerk. He half-turned back to the car, but suddenly, ridiculously, skipped and looked down at his feet, because the water was into his shoes. He swore under his breath and shouted towards the car. "Back her up, Jim," he said. "The water's still rising."

The engine started and the car moved back, and she and the policeman moved back with it. When it stopped, she went right past it and sat down on the dry road and began to pull off her boots to get the water out of them. She emptied the water out and put the wet boots on again over her wet feet. When she stood up, there were two policemen, both standing in front of the car. They stood with their backs to her, staring out across the water. They had turned the headlights off. The car was a black shape, with its side and rear lights glowing in the faint white light from the sky. Away ahead of them, across the widening stretch of water, the lights of Calton still showed. She walked down and stood beside them, looking at the faint lights across the water. They took no notice of her at all.

They stood there in silence for a minute, and then the water drove them back again, and again the car was moved back, and she and the first policeman moved back with it. The driver got out and came to them again where they stood on the edge of the water. "Going to be a big one," he said, and the other nodded.

"Won't last long," he said. "They never do. We'll wait for it. At least he can't get away."

She turned to look at them as they talked, and when she turned again, the lights of Calton were no longer there. She peered into the half-darkness, trying to find them, but could not. She knew then. She knew it was not the water that had put the lights out. It was Matthew Summers who had turned them off, and left all in order at Calton, and gone down to make his bargain with the river.

There was nothing to keep her now. There was nothing to keep the policemen either, but she was not going to tell them that. They would find out soon enough, because the water would go down now. The river would keep its bargain. She turned and walked back towards the car, and as she came to it, the rear door on her side opened, and Steve got out. For a moment they stood and looked at each other in silence. Then he shut the door of the car and walked past her down towards the two policemen. He was going to join them in their watch, and much good would it do him. She would have to deal with him presently, but that was a different problem in a different world. For the moment she had more important things to think about. She grieved for Matthew Summers, but she found, with a sort of compunction but a conscious relief, that it was not a shattering, personal grief. She grieved for the loss of something intrinsically valuable, but he had never been hers, nor she his. They had made love because they had to, but they had never held hands. Above all, she was grateful to him, as in some way she always had been, right from that first evening. He had come when she had needed him most, and now she was her own, as he had told her she must be.

But she felt faint and utterly weary, and her feet were cold, and there was nothing to keep her here. She set off up the road towards the village, walking with a new step.